"If we don't jump into that water we'll die."

"And once we make it to shore?" Ellie asked. "Then what? We're back in the jungle again."

"At least we'll be away from the men after us."

"There's a bounty on my head, Ryan. You don't think they'll find us again?"

"I don't know what other option we have, Ellie."

She blew out a huff of air. "So what's your plan?"

"They're not paying attention to us for the moment, so we jump. Hopefully, they won't notice right away that we're gone. Once we get to the shore...we run."

She looked up at him, her eyes wide with fear, but also the courage he'd noticed before. Emotion washed through him—one he couldn't quite identify. For the first time since Heather's death, he felt something that left him wishing they were somewhere else—anywhere else—where he could get to know her better.

He slammed shut the thought. Now was not the time. He needed to stay focused on getting them out of here. Alive.

Lisa Harris is a Christy Award™ winner and winner of the Best Inspirational Suspense Novel for 2011 from *RT Book Reviews*. She and her family are missionaries in southern Africa. When she's not working, she loves hanging out with her family, cooking different ethnic dishes, photography and heading into the African bush on safari. For more information about her books and life in Africa, visit her website at lisaharriswrites.com.

Books by Lisa Harris

Love Inspired Suspense

No Place to Hide

Lisa Harris

HARLEQUIN® LOVE INSPIRED® SUSPENSE

Recycling programs
for this product may
not exist in your area.

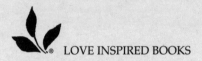 LOVE INSPIRED BOOKS

ISBN-13: 978-1-335-49049-0

No Place to Hide

Copyright © 2018 by Lisa Harris

This edition published by arrangement with Love Inspired Books.

® and TM are trademarks of Love Inspired Books, used under license. Trademarks indicated with ® are registered in the United States Patent and Trademark Office, the Canadian Intellectual Property Office and in other countries.

www.Harlequin.com

Printed in U.S.A.

Fear thou not; for I am with thee:
be not dismayed; for I am thy God: I will strengthen thee;
yea, I will help thee; yea, I will uphold thee
with the right hand of my righteousness.
—*Isaiah* 41:10

To all the wonderful friends I made
while living in this beautiful country.
You will always be a part of who I am today.

ONE

Rio de Janeiro, Brazil

Ellie Webb made her way down the steep incline of the favela, where hundreds of homes sat packed together in a sprawling maze of steep streets and unpaved narrow alleys. While the working-class shantytown was home for thousands of lower-middle-class Brazilians, for her the tight-knit community had become the perfect place to disappear during the day while she taught English to local kids hoping for the chance of a better future. And for her, darker skin, along with an ability to speak fluent Portuguese, had allowed her to blend into the community.

Almost.

She caught the incredible view of Sugarloaf Mountain that sat at the mouth of Guanabara Bay and jutted out into the Atlantic as she headed past a family-run restaurant and dozens of other tiny shops and homes. In reality, she'd never completely fit in, just like she would never be able to forget why she was here. Long days at the center offering outreach programs and development opportunities had helped keep her busy enough to numb the pain, but she still missed her job and her friends. Still wondered if her best friend, Maddie, had found another maid of honor for her September wedding, and how Lucy, her miniature golden retriever, was doing.

Her phone rang, interrupting her thoughts, and she pulled it out of her back pocket, hoping it was Dr. Reynolds letting her know he'd arrived.

"Hello?"

"Ellie? Ellie, I can't believe it's you."

Her heart thudded in her chest. "I'm sorry...who is this?"

"It's Audrey."

"Aunt Audrey? Wait a minute. How did you find me?"

Because it wasn't possible. Her mother's sister was the only family she had left, and yet even Audrey had been told she'd died in the same fire that killed her father. It had meant no communication that might risk Arias's men finding her. No telephone calls or letters. No social media. Nothing that could bring the cartel leader and his hit men back to her. Not until he was back in prison along with whomever he'd hired for the hit.

"I was visiting your father the night he was killed. I saw you run out. I went after you but lost you in all the commotion. After that I...I was so scared they'd come after me." Her aunt paused. "Later when the authorities said you were dead, I couldn't believe it. But I never stopped looking for you."

Ellie stood in the middle of the busy street, barely noticing the group of kids playing an impromptu game of soccer, or the loud hip-hop beat pumping through someone's radio. Because her aunt's revelation was like a punch to the gut. She'd kept her aunt in the dark in order to protect her, but if Audrey knew she was alive, who else did?

She started walking again. "I don't understand."

"I know you don't, and I don't have time to explain right now." Her aunt sounded frantic. Terrified of something. "All you need to know is that I hired a private detective to find you, but he's been murdered. He'd managed to track down your cell phone and where you are, but now I'm afraid that the men who killed him have that information and know where you are. I'm so, so sorry, Ellie, but you need to run."

Ellie's mind fought to untangle her aunt's words. Because nothing made sense. No one besides her father's best friend, Jarrod Kendall, knew where she was. He'd assured her of that, and she trusted him with her life. He'd arranged for her false papers, a visa and even the leak to the media that her body had been discovered in the fire. Which was why everyone believed she was dead.

"Where are you now?" her aunt asked. "Because you need to leave Rio."

"In the favela where I work. I was on my way to grab lunch for my team—"

"You can't go back to your work or to your apartment."

Ellie bit back the list of questions she needed to ask and looked behind her, feeling vulnerable even in the middle of the crowded favela. How had a private detective managed to track her down?

"How much time do I have?" she asked her aunt.

"Not long. They have the same information I do, which means they could be there right now."

A sick feeling spread through her.

"Then I've got to go," Ellie said. "I'll call as soon as I can."

She forced her mind to click through her options. If her aunt was right, then she couldn't go back to the center where she worked. Nor could she go home or to any of her friends here. She was going to have to disappear. Again. The familiar sense of fear she'd lived with over the past few months washed through her. She had no reason not to trust her aunt. Unless someone had gotten to her as well.

Ellie hurried down a narrow flight of cement stairs, past a woman hanging up her laundry. A young girl swept the walk outside her house. Children played in the narrow thoroughfare with graffiti on the walls.

She glanced behind her up the alley. There was no way they could find her here. Was there? A man in black jeans and a white T-shirt darted down the stairs behind her, almost knocking down one of the kids who was playing. His cold gaze caught hers as he headed toward her.

They'd found her.

Ellie smashed the cell phone against the pavement, then started running, careful not to lose her balance on the uneven pavement as she raced down the street. Her aunt had been right. Going back to her apartment wasn't an option. She had her passport and some cash with her in her leather messenger bag. Now she just needed to get to the bus terminal, where she'd left a bugout bag in one of the long-term lockers in case something like this happened, and leave the city.

She turned down another street, then glanced behind her, unsure if she'd lost the guy with all the pedestrian traffic. No…he was still coming toward her. She needed a way out. A motorcycle sat fifty feet ahead of her. There was something familiar about the tall, muscular driver who had turned around to see what the commotion was.

Ryan Kendall?

The last time she remembered seeing him was on a trip to his family ranch well over a decade ago, where he'd driven her crazy with his dumb jokes and juvenile pranks.

"Hurry," he shouted, handing her a helmet.

There was no time to ask what Jarrod Kendall's son was doing here. Instead, she jumped on the back of the seat, grabbed onto his waist and shouted for him to go. He zipped around a group of women, then headed for the main road as her pursuer disappeared behind them.

A minute later, Ellie's heart was still pounding as Ryan merged into the traffic. She closed her eyes, wrapping her arms tighter around his waist as he took the turn too fast for her comfort. It was one thing sitting behind a *mototaxi* driver who knew the streets of Rio like the back of his hand. She was quite sure Ryan, on the other hand, would be completely lost without his rented GPS.

He sped down the freeway like a local, but even that didn't help loosen the knots in her stomach as she pressed against his back. It wasn't rush hour, but the traffic was still congested. Someone honked behind them. She tried to slow her breathing. She knew that Arias's operation was extensive, though Ryan's father had assured her that she'd be out of Arias's reach here in Rio. Apparently, that wasn't true. All she wanted right now was to find somewhere safe, where they couldn't get to her.

But they'd just proved that place didn't exist.

Ellie glanced behind her, unable to shake the uneasiness that had settled over her. The surrounding mountains boxed in the city, helping to add to the congested traffic, which was why she always took a taxi in order to avoid driving. Something in her peripheral vision caught her eye. A motorcycle was weaving in and out of traffic as it sped toward them. If it was the same guy she'd caught coming after her in the favela... She squeezed her arms tighter around Ryan's waist as they flew past a large truck.

"You okay?" Ryan shouted above the noise of the busy freeway.

"No." She leaned against him and squeezed her eyes shut for a moment. "I think we're being followed."

Ryan glanced in the side mirror at the motorcycle closing in behind them. He couldn't help but wonder for a split second how he'd managed to find himself speeding down a highway in the middle of Rio with a possible cartel member behind him, instead of scuba diving in the middle of the Atlantic like he'd planned. He sped up, then weaved in between two cars, trying to determine if Ellie's theory was correct. But the other motorcycle also increased its speed and continued to bridge the distance between them.

Definitely not a coincidence.

He glanced in his side mirror again, trying to deduce what the other rider was planning to do. Running them off the road was always a possibility. Or maybe he'd simply been planning to follow them and hadn't expected to be made. Ellie's arms squeezed tighter around his waist, making him wonder what he'd been thinking when he'd impulsively rented the motorcycle. There was nothing heroic about rescuing a maiden in distress only to throw her into another life-threatening situation.

The back window of the car to their right shattered. Ryan swerved to miss hitting the car as it fishtailed, and almost ran into a single-cab truck before the car hit the center barrier, then skidded to a stop behind them.

But there was no way they could stop. The armed motorcyclist had just made his intentions perfectly clear.

"Hold on." Ryan pressed on the accelerator, praying as he worked to stretch out the gap between them. "We need to lose him."

"There's a split in the highway up ahead," she shouted. "A mile, maybe two. We might be able to lose him."

"Which direction should I go?"

"To the left. The other way veers off into a sharp curve."

It wasn't a foolproof plan, but it was going to have to work. He continued to increase his speed, dodging in front of cars as he tried to widen the distance between them, but the other motorcycle still managed to keep up with them.

If he took a shot at them again…

A minute later, they passed a sign, signaling the upcoming split. Two kilometers, or roughly one mile. Traffic was fairly heavy, but he maneuvered through the lanes, keeping primarily to the right, as if he was planning to exit. He kept his eyes on his mirrors. He'd raced motorcycles all through high school and college and had been good at it. His father had been the one who'd taught him everything, from running tighter lines, to how to use the brakes, to ensuring he understood every minute detail of how a bike ran. And that attention to detail had translated into winning more races.

But this was different. Back then he hadn't been riding with someone holding on to him he was supposed to protect with a shooter closing in.

He passed another sign as he weaved through traffic, then went back into the right lane. Another half mile to the split. He held his position, waiting until the last minute, then swerved to the left, barely making the turn.

The other bike tried to follow, but by the time he realized what they'd done, it was too late. The driver swerved to the left, overcompensating, then slid across several lanes of traffic before disappearing from view.

They road in silence for another thirty minutes, until he was certain they weren't being followed. He turned onto an avenue running parallel to the Atlantic Ocean, then found a place to park the bike. With dozens of tourists and locals enjoying the warm October sunshine along the white, sandy shoreline, they would be safe here for the moment.

He helped Ellie off the bike, then pulled off his helmet, his hands shaking as he set it on the seat. If his hands were shaking, he could only imagine what she was feeling. Not only had they just survived a near fatal accident, but this entire situation was also intensely personal for her. She'd lost her father, and now, once again, almost her life.

She pulled off her helmet, then caught his gaze. "Thanks for the rescue, but what are you doing in Rio?"

He hesitated at her question. "I was working off the coast, and my father sent me to check on you. Said that the last time you spoke to him you'd sounded upset. He wanted to make sure you were okay."

"I guess my paranoia that the cartel would find me wasn't that far off." Her eyes watered as she blew out a sharp breath. "My aunt called right before you showed up. Warned me that Arias's men had found me."

He shook his head. "Wait a minute… No one is supposed to even know you're alive, and yet we just got shot at and almost run off the road, and now you're telling me that your aunt knows where you are as well."

"She's been looking for me."

Her watery eyes turned into full-blown tears, and he had no idea how to react to her crying. Hugging her seemed too intimate, and yet he didn't want to just ignore what she was feeling. The last time he'd seen her, she'd been fourteen or fifteen. They used to spend summers at his father's Colorado ranch, until her family moved to Dallas. And now his father had sent him to do a simple extraction, but he had a feeling this was going to turn out to be a bit more complicated.

"Are you okay?" he asked.

"I will be." She wiped her cheek with the back of her hand, clearly trying to gain back her composure. "I'm sorry. Except for the night my father was murdered, I don't think I've ever been so terrified."

"You have nothing to be sorry about, but we need to get you out of the country," he said. "My father's already booked two seats on a direct flight to the States for tonight in case I felt we needed to leave immediately, which clearly we do."

He focused his attention on her but continued to stay fully aware of the scene around him. He couldn't assume anything when it came to their safety. Not after what he'd just witnessed.

"Ellie…"

She stared out across the stunning blue water lined with countless kiosks and beachgoers a few seconds longer before looking up at him. "I'm sorry, but I can't leave."

"What are you talking about?" he asked. "We were almost killed a few minutes ago."

Surely he'd misunderstood her.

"I have information on the man behind my father's death," she said. "Proof that could finally lead to his arrest and conviction."

"What kind of proof?" he asked, unsure he liked the direction of the conversation. She couldn't be planning to play detective and try to solve her father's murder herself. He'd agreed to escort her home. Not follow up on some clue she thought she'd come up with. *That* he planned to leave to the authorities.

"I made contact with a doctor who works in the north of Brazil along the Amazon River," she said quickly. "He has evidence he's been afraid to take to the authorities, but he's agreed to meet with me."

"Wait a minute…so you're planning to go to the Amazon?"

"I've already booked a private flight that leaves in the morning."

Ryan frowned. A simple extraction, in and out, didn't include a stop in the Amazon.

"I'm sorry, but you can't—"

"If they can find me here in Brazil," she said, catching his gaze, "what's to stop them from finding me back in the US, where they have even more resources? Which means I won't be able to quit running until the men behind my father's death are in prison."

Ryan shook his head. "I agreed to take you back to the US, not off on some wild-goose chase down the Amazon."

"That's fine, because I'm not asking you to go with me." She let out a sharp breath. "Have you ever lost someone you loved?"

Ryan's muscles stiffened at the question. "Yes, but—"

"Then you have to understand that not only do I need closure to my father's death, I need the men who killed him to pay for what they did. And if I ever want to stop running, I have to make sure they're caught."

"And some…doctor in the Amazon is your best lead? How does that play in to your father's murder?"

"Let's just say that even cartel leaders and drug lords need medical care."

"And this doctor you tracked down knows the man you believe is behind your father's death and has some kind of information you believe might help solve his case?"

"Exactly."

"Which could put his life in danger as well."

"I know, but we've been very careful," she said. "He works one week a month at a second clinic about two hours upriver of where he lives. He's agreed to meet me there. No one will suspect anything."

"Forget it. It's way too dangerous, and I promised my father I'd get you out of here." Ryan glanced down the wide boulevard that ran parallel to the ocean and was lined with hotels, restaurants and bars. How was he supposed to convince her to leave? "Listen. I'm not a chauvinist, but a woman on her own, traveling down the Amazon, is probably not the best idea. Especially when the cartel is looking for you."

"Don't you think I haven't thought of that?" Ellie looked up at him. "I realize this isn't some sanitized cruise, and we're not just talking about avoiding leeches and piranhas. It's not safe. I get it. And in fact, I feel as if I'm poking my finger into a hornet's nest."

He didn't miss the apprehension in her voice or the hint of fear in her eyes as she caught his gaze. But he also didn't miss the look of fierce determination. The bottom line, though, was that someone was out there, looking for her, and from what his father had told him, they weren't going to stop until they found her.

"You know my father," he said. "He will do everything in his power to stop whoever's behind this. Including finding out what this doctor knows. But you don't have to do this on your own. It's not safe. We need to get to the airport and return to the States."

She shook her head. "You don't understand. You don't have to come with me, but I'm going."

TWO

Ellie started walking away from him, toward the water, still carrying the helmet she'd been wearing. She needed to clear her head. She wished she didn't feel so angry. Wished her nerves weren't so rattled. Surely flying to the Amazon to meet the doctor wasn't nearly as dangerous as riding a motorcycle across Rio with Ryan Kendall. Unless, of course, the cartel managed to track her there as well.

Memories engulfed her, dragging her back to a place she didn't want to be. Like the last time she'd spoken to her father. He'd apologized for burdening her with his problems, telling her that this case had him on edge, and with the evidence he'd seen, he was ready to give his judgment and see Mauricio Arias remain in prison for the rest of his life. It might not have been the first time he'd received threats, but for some reason, when she'd hung up the phone, she'd been left with the impression that this time was different. This time it was personal.

She had already been worried over the toll the case had been taking on his health, which was why she'd insisted on coming over and making dinner. Normally their weekly Friday-night dinners included takeout and a couple hours of conversation, where they were forbidden to mention politics or law. But after the week her father had had, she'd figured he'd enjoy a home-cooked meal rather than spicy Thai or greasy pizza.

Instead, she'd found her father in the entryway. He was lying on the hardwood floor, a pool of blood beneath him, and his eyes were closed, as if he was sleeping.

Except he hadn't been sleeping.

She'd knelt over her father and quickly felt for a pulse or a breath—anything that would assure her it wasn't too late. She'd begged that God would step in and wake her up from this nightmare. Her stomach had twisted as she pulled back his suit jacket, revealing where the bullet had struck his chest. Everything her father had feared had become a reality.

A second later, a bullet had slammed into the wall behind her. She'd glanced at the figure standing in the doorway on the other side of the room as time seemed to momentarily freeze. Dark hair, piercing brown eyes, spiderweb tat on the side of his neck… Details imprinted on her mind as she'd grabbed her phone, then dived behind the paisley couch. A second bullet had struck the arm of the piece of furniture, missing her by only a couple inches. Her father was still lying motionless on the floor, but there had been nothing else she could have done for him. He was already gone. Which meant she'd had to find a way out of the house before it was too late.

She tried to shake off the memories that had yet to stop chasing her the past couple months as she walked past a beach vendor selling coconut water straight from the coconut to a couple of tourists. On any other day, Copacabana Beach, with its long stretch of shoreline, crystal blue waters and the magnificent Sugarloaf Mountain in the background, was one of her favorite places in the city. But today, she didn't really see any of it.

How was she supposed to make Ryan understand she couldn't return with him?

She stopped at the edge of the sand, not far from where a father and son were building a sandcastle. She and Ryan always had been polar opposites growing up. His father had mentioned that he'd spent a decade as a navy diver and now worked as a saturation diver for oil companies. She wasn't sure what the job entailed, but she was pretty sure it was dangerous. She definitely wasn't the adventurous type, but this wasn't the time to admit to him how terrified she felt. If she did, she had a feeling he'd kidnap her himself in order to get her to return.

But the risks involved didn't change anything. Not now.

"Ellie…"

She felt a surge of resolve run through her as he stepped up next to her. She studied his lean, solid profile, stopping at his strong jawline and five-o'clock shadow. She trusted him, but only because she trusted his father, and his father had sent him. She also knew that flying to the Amazon hadn't been a part of the bargain. But until the authorities found her father's killer, she'd always be looking over her shoulder, and that wasn't a life she intended to live any longer. Which was why she had no plans of backing down. With or without his help.

"I need to find out the truth," she said, "because I'm

tired of running. Nor can I simply ignore the information the doctor has."

She caught the hesitation in his eyes, knowing they needed to leave. Even if they had managed to evade the man who'd tried to grab her in the favela, they were still out in the open and exposed. But this wasn't a fight she was willing to walk away from.

"I'm sorry, but I can't let you do that," he said. "Once we get to the safe house back in the States, you can meet with my father and tell him about this doctor and the information he has. I'm sure he'll be willing to send someone to meet with the man."

The warm sun made her long to take off her shoes and dig her toes into the sand, as if it was just a normal day. "That's not good enough. Dr. Reynolds is risking his life to meet with me, which means I owe it to both him and my father to go speak to him. And he told me that he'll only meet with me. Not the authorities."

"Are you forgetting that not only did your aunt manage to track down your cell phone number and location, we were just chased out of the favela?"

"I know it sounds crazy, but I need to show you something." She pulled a couple photos out of the side pocket of her bag, desperate for him to understand. "This is my father a couple months before he was killed. He was a huge sports fan, and I surprised him with tickets to watch the Dallas Mavericks for his birthday. And this—" she showed him the second photo "—this is the sketch I drew of the man who killed my father, then burned down his house."

Ryan let out a soft sigh. "My father told me about what happened, and I am truly sorry for your loss."

"What exactly did he tell you?" she asked.

"That three months ago your father was murdered by members of the cartel and his house was burned down in connection to a high-profile case he was presiding over. And that you were a witness to who murdered him—and despite what the news channels all reported, you were very much alive."

Except for Ryan's father, she hadn't spoken to anyone about that day. Her friends back in the United States thought she was dead, and her new friends here couldn't find out what had happened to her. It was a burden she'd had to face on her own with only her faith to carry her through.

"The last time I spoke with my father," she continued, "he sounded distracted. Preoccupied. He'd hinted about the strain of the cartel-related triple homicide. When I pressed him for more information, he assured me nothing was wrong, but I didn't believe him. Especially when he admitted there was missing evidence and a string of threats directed toward him.

"The next day, I found him lying in the entryway of his house in a pool of blood." She fought back the emotion as she looked up at Ryan. "I don't need a sketch to remember what his murderer looked like, because I see him every night when I close my eyes to go to sleep, and every time I'm reminded of why I'm here. Your father helped me disappear. Helped leak the rumor to the media that I'd died in the fire so the cartel wouldn't come after me. And yet even that didn't stop them from looking for me."

"Why don't you contact the authorities and tell them what's happening?" he asked.

She ignored the string of vendors heading their way with offers of ice cream, skewers of shrimp and henna tattoos. "Because there's a leak somewhere in the investigation, and besides your father, I still don't know who I can trust. Your father's been trying to figure out the truth, but he's walking a fine line, and so far, he hasn't been able to."

"You have to understand that I'm truly sorry for everything that has happened to you," Ryan said, motioning to the men that they weren't interested in buying anything. "But my father sent me here to ensure your safety. Not to take you on some wild-goose chase that may or may not pay off."

"And I need you to understand why I have to stay and find out the truth."

"I do, but—"

"No. I don't think you do understand. Arias is known for his brutality. He has people working for him—hired to do his dirty work—along with people he pays in order to ensure he walks, which is why my father is dead. And why I'll be dead as well if he gets his way."

"I get that, but you and I aren't equipped to carry out an investigation. What you just told me about Arias should be reason enough for both of us to get as far from here as possible."

"So, what? I just keep running. Keep playing this game of cat and mouse until someone finds my dead body and he gets away with murder again. He knows I'm alive."

"No. Of course not—"

"That's why I need to meet with the doctor."

Today, Ryan Kendall might not be the irritating teenager she remembered—after all, he had just shown up unexpectedly and rescued her—but he was still just as stubborn. And so was she, and she had no intention of changing her mind.

"I need you to take me to the bus station," she said, heading back toward the bike.

Ryan hurried to catch up with her. "Why?"

"I decided that if I ever needed to get out quickly, I was going to be ready this time. I've got a bugout bag in one of the lockers with some things I'll need, including a burn phone. I'll stay at a hotel tonight, then take a taxi to the airstrip in the morning."

"And this contact you're supposed to meet with, this doctor. Where are you meeting him?"

"I've got a pilot flying me to an airstrip that's located near the small village where he'll be."

"I'm coming with you."

She stopped, turned around, then quickly stepped out of the way of a couple of kids. "I'm not asking you to come with me."

"Maybe not, and while I'll probably regret this, I'm volunteering. But on one condition. Once you talk to the doctor, you have to promise you'll leave with me. And in the meantime," he said, "we're going to have to find a way to keep you safe."

Ryan frowned as they headed back toward the motorcycle, certain he was going to regret what he'd just agreed to. He still wasn't sure why he'd offered to go with her to the Amazon despite undeniable evidence that someone was after her. So much for his father's clear-cut plan to simply escort her back to the United States to the safe house he was setting up.

But one of her questions had struck a chord, making it impossible for him to just walk away. He glanced at the watch Heather had given him a month before their wedding. Two weeks before she'd died. He knew all too well how hard it was to have someone you love snatched away from you with no warning. And how important it was to find the answers that would bring closure. Even if it meant risking everything. Heather would have told him to go. Just like she would have already told him to let her go.

He glanced behind them, still unable to shake the uneasiness. Someone was still out there looking for them. He needed to keep her safe, but they'd tracked her to the favela. Who was to say they couldn't track her to the Amazon?

"You know you don't have to do this," she said as they stepped up next to the bike.

"Don't you even start trying to talk me out of this," he said, slipping on his helmet.

She smiled for the first time. "Thank you for coming with me."

"Just doing what my father asked and keeping you safe."

He took a few seconds to study her as he pushed the strap down under his chin. Shoulder-length dark hair. Warm smile. Wide almond-colored eyes. She'd turned out incredibly beautiful.

Not that it mattered.

What mattered was getting them both out of here in one piece.

Thirty minutes later Ryan pulled into the parking garage that was attached to the bus terminal. Outside the busy station, scores of people bustled about, surrounded by yellow taxis. Ryan watched a couple lug a suitcase out of the trunk of their car as he and Ellie headed through the garage. Three tourists with backpacks were heading toward the terminal in front of them. He forced himself to shake the worry. No one had followed them here, and no one was going to follow them to the Amazon. They'd fly in, meet the doctor and fly out.

Simple.

He might not have been able to save Heather, but he was going to save Ellie.

"Do you remember the last time we saw each other?" he asked, pushing the lingering memories away as they started across the catwalk that had access to the upper boarding sector of the bus terminal.

"It was the summer before I started eighth grade if I remember correctly," she said.

He had a feeling she hadn't forgotten. Her family had visited his parents' ranch, and Ryan had dared her to jump off the roof and into the swimming pool. She must have gotten tired of his taunts, because she'd eventually climbed onto that roof before propelling herself into the deep end of the pool below.

It hadn't ended well. She'd panicked and his father had ended up jumping into the pool and rescuing her.

"I was thinking I probably owed you an apology," he said.

"Forget it. That was a long time ago, though I did think I was going to drown that day. And for the record, I now have an irrational fear of drowning."

"Like I said, I owe you an apology, though I have grown up since then in case you were wondering."

She smiled, but he could still sense the tension in her stride. He'd hoped that breaking the ice between them would help her relax, but she'd been right when she'd told him that this wasn't some exotic holiday. Neither of them had any idea what was going to be waiting for them once they arrived. Which meant he was going to have to be prepared for anything.

Inside, the crowded terminal looked more like a shopping center, with its dozens of shops and food vendors. But while there might be safety in numbers, he also knew that whoever was after her would probably assume she was going to try to leave the city. And Rio's main bus terminal was as good as anyplace to start surveying. He searched the crowded space for anyone who looked out of place. Someone without any luggage, or someone he'd seen earlier today. But the odds were in their favor. They might know she was in Rio, but Arias's men couldn't keep tabs on every plane, bus and car exiting the city.

"Just give me a minute," she said as they approached the lockers. "I need to pay, then grab my bag."

His cell phone rang as they stepped in front of the lockers. He checked the caller ID. It was his father.

"Did you find her?" his father asked.

"Yeah. I was just getting ready to call you."

"And...?"

Ryan turned around, hesitating with his answer. "They know she's here in Rio. A guy was after her, and we barely made it out of the favela."

"Ryan, you need to get out of there now. Everything's

arranged on my end with the safe house. Get to the airport. You'll be safe there until your flight—"

"It's not going to be quite that simple." He glanced at Ellie, who was busy paying for the locker rental. His father might have trusted him to get her to safety, but he wasn't going to be happy when he heard they wouldn't be making the flight back to the United States.

"Ryan…what's going on?"

"She's arranged a private flight to the Amazon. She's been in contact with someone she believes has information on her father's killer. Evidence that could potentially help take down Arias. She's insisting on meeting with him tomorrow."

"Forget it. I don't care what she's found at this point. You need to get her out now. It's not safe where you are."

"And if she's determined to go?" Ryan pressed his phone against his ear in order to hear better in the noisy terminal. "I can't just let her fly out on her own—"

"I promised her father if anything ever happened to him I'd take care of her. He would have done the same thing for you or your sister."

"I told her I'd go with her."

"Then tell her you changed your mind. I don't care if you have to drag her to the airport, you get her on that plane, Ryan. Do you understand me?"

"I can try, but I can't make any promises."

Ryan hung up as Ellie walked up to him with a large, gray backpack hanging off her shoulder.

"Is everything okay?" she asked.

He slid his phone into his front pocket. "That was my father."

"He doesn't want me going, does he?"

"No."

She shifted the backpack on her shoulder. "Your father's done a lot for me, but I'm not going to change my mind. My contact knows what he's up against and has made it very clear that he won't speak with anyone else. I can't lose this opportunity to find out the truth."

He pulled her out of the way of a group of travelers who weren't paying attention to where they were going, and felt her jump at his touch.

"I'm sorry," she said. "My nerves are on edge."

"Which is why my father is right. These people who are after you…they aren't going to stop looking. We could fly your contact somewhere safe until this is over, or—"

"He won't meet with anyone else, but I'll understand if you want to change your mind about coming with me."

"When I said I'd come with you, I meant it," he said as they started back to the parking garage. "We can get a couple rooms at a secure hotel I know about, and leave in the morning."

"And your father?" she asked.

"Don't worry about it. I'll deal with him later."

Because in the meantime he had plenty of other things to worry about. He knew enough about Arias and the cartel to realize they were about to walk into a war zone. Her father's death was related to the cartel. All along the Amazon were drug gangs, cartel leaders and even pirates, all on the rise due to rapid changes throughout the area. A surging population paired with organized crime had helped to fuel a sense of lawlessness. And they were headed right into the middle of it.

THREE

At seven thirty the next morning, Ellie and Ryan sat in the small waiting room adjacent to the hangar while their pilot filled out the necessary paperwork for their flight. Perspiration had beaded across the back of her neck, making her wish the stuffy room had an air conditioner, or if nothing else a fan to circulate the air. Even though they were just easing into summer, today's temperatures were supposed to hit eighty degrees with high humidity. Along the Amazon, the temperatures would probably be even higher.

While she honestly hadn't expected him to go with her, Ryan had already gone far beyond the call of duty. He'd secured two rooms for them at a hotel, where they'd ordered room service to ensure no one saw them. But as much as she'd wanted to catch up with him, she'd been too exhausted emotionally to be very sociable. By nine, she'd fallen into a restless sleep filled with nightmares of someone chasing her through the Amazon rain forest.

She yawned, then glanced at her phone for the umpteenth time, stood up and started pacing the VIP departure lounge. Her determination to follow through with their plan wavered. Maybe Ryan and his father had been right, and they should have taken last night's flight back to the United States. She had no experience in tracking down a killer. Which was why she should leave the investigation to the authorities and trust that they would find out the truth as to who had killed her father. Just like the legal process would—at some point—put them in prison, where they belonged. All she was doing now was risking the lives of both Dr. Reynolds and Ryan.

"Ellie…what's wrong?"

She glanced at her phone again, the familiar worry gnawing at her gut. "I'm hoping nothing, but I still haven't heard from Dr. Reynolds. I texted him this new number. He was supposed to send me a signal when he arrived this morning so I knew he was okay."

"I wouldn't worry. Things run slower in this part of the world and never keep to a schedule. Which means there could be any number of explanations. The boat he's on could have broken down, he might simply be running late—"

"Or they could have gotten to him." She turned around and faced Ryan, his casual answer doing little to reassure her. "I'm sorry, but I'm the one who dragged him into this mess and if anything happens to him…"

Ryan leaned forward and rested his forearms against his thighs. "From what you've already told me, the doctor made his own decision to gather information against the cartel, which means I'd say he did a pretty good job of dragging himself into this situation on his own."

"I know. But while I'm not the only person affected by Arias, this has become personal. I need to find a way to put an end to it." She sat back down next to him. "My father's dead, my aunt thought I was dead, too, and all my friends and the people I worked with think I died in that fire. I just want this all to be over."

"That's why we're going," he said, catching her gaze. "It will be. Soon. I promise."

"The two of you ready to go?" The pilot she'd hired stepped into the room, interrupting their conversation.

She nodded at the balding man in his early fifties, praying that the trip that had eaten up most of her savings would be worth it. Ryan grabbed his small backpack and walked with her toward the plane as she shoved aside any second thoughts. If it meant bringing her father's murderer to justice, she could do this.

Fifteen minutes later, while the small craft was heading north above the city, Ellie stared out the window. The blue-green ocean was to the right, running along Rio's skyline surrounded by the mountain chain that ran along the coast of South America. She loved flying. Loved the feeling of climbing to altitude, then soaring across the miniature images below.

It was almost enough to make her temporarily forget where they were going and why. She took in a slow, deep breath, and for the first time in weeks she felt her muscles begin to relax. Maybe it was simply the calm before the storm, but even if that was all it was, it was a moment she intended to hold on to for as long as she could. In another four hours or so, they'd be on the ground, and she'd have to deal again with the reality of her situation and how someone wanted her dead.

She glanced at Ryan with those striking blue eyes of his. He sat beside her, mouth tight, hands clasped tightly in his lap. Her brow furrowed. She would never have pegged him for someone with a phobia of flying.

"Not much of a flyer?" she asked.

"I don't mind flying, actually. I just hate the takeoffs and landings," he said, opening his eyes and shooting her a grin. "I know it doesn't make sense, but I've always preferred to be under the water, for some reason, than thousands of feet above it."

She chuckled, enjoying talking with him after the awkwardness of yesterday seemed to have passed. "Your father mentioned you used to be a diver for the navy. That sounds a lot more frightening—and more dangerous—than flying."

"I left the navy after about a decade and now work as a saturation diver."

"Your father told me that's what you're doing now, but he didn't really explain what the job was."

"I work for oil companies using a saturation system. We live in a pressurized chamber for up to a month, then are transported to the underwater work area every day in a closed bell."

"A closed bell?" She felt a shiver slide through her. "So you live and work under constant pressure?"

"It allows more work to be done efficiently without worrying about decompression stops."

She shook her head. "I'm sorry, but that definitely sounds terrifying."

He shot her a smile. "It's intense work, but the old Jacques Cousteau documentaries always fascinated me as a kid. Whenever we were on holiday, I would be out spearfishing or snorkeling. I was always in the sea and always wanted to be a diver. Back then I just had no idea I could make money doing it."

She let out another soft laugh. At least he was human with at least one irrational fear. And there was another thing she was pretty certain about as well. His presence was one of the reasons she hadn't completely fallen apart. Over the past three months she'd had to deal with not only the death of her father, but also the complete upheaval of her life. And while she'd made friends here in Brazil, she hadn't been able to tell them the real reason she was here. Regular check-ins with Ryan's father had helped, but he was five thousand miles away.

"I thought my father told me you were married," she said as the plane leveled off and his hands began to relax in his lap. No ring had made her assume otherwise.

"Married? No." His brow rose slightly at the question. "That would be my sister. She got married right out of college and now has three little girls."

"So you never found Ms. Right?" She'd asked the question as a simple conversation starter, but from the look on his face, she'd just wandered into forbidden territory. "I'm sorry if that was too personal."

"I was engaged. Once." He stared past her out the window.

Yeah...definitely too personal.

Though honestly, she couldn't imagine marrying someone with such a risky job, who was gone for weeks at a time. More than likely his ex had decided to find someone with a more...normal day job.

"What about you?" he asked, shifting the subject. "Any Mr. Right in your life?"

"No, though I was almost engaged once."

Ellie frowned. *That is if you could call wishful thinking almost engaged.* The night she'd expected Lance to propose, he'd broken up with her. And to make it worse, he'd ended up marrying one of her best friends.

She stared back out the window, wondering how she'd allowed their conversation to become so personal. Maybe it was simply having to adjust to the lack of contact with any other Americans over the past few months that had allowed her to let down her guard now. But just because she was lonely didn't mean she was ready to open up her heart.

Ryan settled back in his chair as their pilot leveled out the small plane, leaving the city behind them. Despite her personal questions, he hadn't failed to notice how guarded she seemed. Though he couldn't really blame her. She'd been in hiding for the past three months, without being able to communicate with anyone she cared about.

As for himself, this was already probably the most amount of time he'd spent around a woman for, well... for a very long time. His father was constantly trying to nudge him back into the dating game, and if he didn't know better, he could easily believe his dad had set up this entire scenario to get the two of them together. In fact, a part of him wasn't sure why he hadn't started dating again. Enough time had passed for the major wounds of his heart to begin to heal. But something had still continued to hold him back and keep him running.

Just like Ellie.

Except Ellie had been running from a legitimate threat. From a man who wanted her dead because of retaliation over what she'd seen. He, on the other hand, had been running from his own emotions and fears.

The thought struck him hard. The revelation would no doubt be one his father would be proud of. If he was to start dating again—which he had no plans whatsoever to do—and if he was honest with himself, from the short time he'd been around her, he knew Ellie was the kind of woman he'd like to spend time getting to know better. When they were kids, he'd enjoyed hanging out with her, and she'd always been a good sport no matter how much he'd teased her.

"Where'd you learn Portuguese?" he asked, figuring they could both do with a neutral subject.

"I love languages and ended up studying both Spanish and Portuguese in high school and college. Right after I graduated, I was given an incredible opportunity to work for two years in a studio based in São Paulo. I ended up fluent in the language and loved my time here. So when my father was murdered, it seemed like the perfect place to disappear. And it would have been if Arias's arm didn't stretch further than we thought. I never imagined he could find me here."

He watched her smile fade into a frown. The underlying reason they were here had once again managed to rear its ugly head.

"Sorry. I promised myself I wouldn't think about the reason we're going during the flight," she said, "but I can't seem to get away from it."

"It's hard to ignore."

"Have I thanked you for coming with me?" she asked.

He smiled. "Once or twice."

"I know this plan probably seems crazy, and trust me, I typically tend to avoid crazy."

"Like jumping off the roof into a swimming pool?" He nudged her with his elbow.

She laughed. "I guess sometimes you can't avoid crazy."

They spent the next couple of hours chatting off and on about what had happened since they'd last seen each other. But never—he noted—about anything too personal. Her job as a medical illustrator, places they'd traveled, his last diving stint, the last books they'd read... And if the conversation started veering toward something personal, she always changed the subject.

Ellie glanced out the window, then grabbed his arm. "Look down below us."

"What is it?"

"About four or five miles from Manaus, two tributaries of the Amazon meet but don't mix."

"What?" he said as he leaned over her. But she was right. The two colors of the merging rivers were clearly distinct.

"The lighter-colored river is the Solimões," she said. "The darker side of the water is the Rio Negro. Its black-tea color comes from decayed plant matter, and with barely any sediment, it's actually considered one of the cleanest natural waterways on the planet."

"Wow...that is amazing," he said, staring out the window at the water below them. "Though I am curious why they don't they mix."

"Because of the extreme differences in water temperature, density and speed, they stay separate until they hit a strong wave of whitewater and become a part of the Lower Amazon River. I know you've traveled a lot for your job, but I'm guessing you've never visited the Amazon."

"I've worked in Eastern Europe, Australia, South America and the Middle East…but never visited the Amazon."

"Do you see yourself involved in saturation diving long-term?" she asked.

"Probably not." He didn't even have to think about his answer.

"Why not?"

"Other than the fact that it's an extremely demanding job? I think about having a family one day and, despite the money, would prefer not to be away for weeks on end."

She looked back down at the river as the pilot made an announcement through his headset that they would be landing in about fifteen minutes.

"Where exactly are we landing?" Ryan asked, feeling the plane begin to drop in altitude.

"There's a small, isolated airstrip where a contact is supposed to meet us and take us to Dr. Reynolds."

"Is the pilot waiting for us on the ground?"

"He'll return in the morning. I didn't know how long it would take with the doctor, so I thought it was better to stay the night. It will be rustic—"

"You've forgotten I'm pretty used to the simple life," he said. "On the job—when I'm not working—I'm sleeping, eating and relaxing in a tiny pressurized chamber. Let's just say it's about as far from glamorous as you can get."

At half past one, just as the pilot had announced,

they were taxiing down the short runway in the middle
of the dense tropical forest they'd been flying over the
past few hours. Ryan waited for the pilot to open the
side door, then stepped out of the plane behind Ellie,
thankful they'd arrived. Because the sooner they could
talk to the doctor, the sooner they could get out of here.

Ellie picked up her backpack, then turned to their
pilot. "We'll plan to meet at nine in the morning."

The pilot tugged on the waist of his pants. "I'm sorry,
but I won't be able to return tomorrow."

"Wait a minute… What do you mean? That's what
we agreed to."

"Things have changed." The man glanced toward
the tree line behind them. "Turns out you weren't my
highest-paying customer today."

Ryan turned around. Three armed men started toward them. Adrenaline surged as instinct kicked in, and
Ryan's mind quickly ran through their limited options.
His job required him to be able to stay calm in order
to cope with emergencies. But while his gut wanted to
jump in and fight them off, he knew there was no way
he'd win. One of the men quickly grabbed his arm, ensuring he didn't question his decision.

"Ryan…"

Another man grabbed Ellie's arm and told her to shut
up. How had he not seen this coming?

The pilot took an envelope from their leader, then
boarded the plane.

"Wait!" Ryan said, shouting at the pilot. "You can't
just leave us here."

The man holding him back tightened his grip on
Ryan's arm, his protests lost in the roar of the engine.

FOUR

Ellie watched as Ryan lunged toward the man holding him. But the odds were stacked against them.

A rifle clicked next to Ryan's temple. "I wouldn't do that if I were you."

The man dug his fingers deeper into her arm. She'd have a nasty mark above her elbow tomorrow, but if they didn't find a way out of here, a bruise was going to be the least of her problems.

She glanced at Ryan, and the horror that she was the one who'd gotten him into this slowly sank in. She should have listened to his father. Or at the least should have insisted he drop her off at the private airfield, then take his own flight back to the United States.

Except then she'd have been on her own.

She watched as the airplane that had once been their ticket out of here taxied down the runway. It picked up speed, took off, then skimmed the top of the tree line before fading into the white clouds above them. She'd missed something. No one was supposed to have known about her meeting with Dr. Reynolds. She'd made sure of that. And now, not just her and Ryan's lives were at stake, but the doctor's was, too.

"Welcome to the Amazon." One of the armed men with a row of tattoos running down his neck smiled, revealing a large gap between his front teeth.

"This isn't exactly the welcome we expected," Ryan said.

"Your plans have changed, though I am assuming you have already figured that out."

The man ran his finger down her cheek. Ellie pulled back as far as she could, her stomach souring at the smell of alcohol.

"Let her go," Ryan said.

"You're not exactly in a position to argue with me."

"Yuri? I could put an end to this right now. Teach him a lesson." One of the other men aimed his gun at Ryan, the look in his eye making his intent clear.

"If I were you," Yuri said, "I would do what he says. Pedro, he is a bit…trigger-happy, as I think you Americans call it."

"Then just tell me this," Ellie said, searching for answers as to what went wrong. "Who's paying you to take us?"

"I am just the middleman, but don't worry. All of your questions will be answered before long."

He barked out a string of orders in Portuguese.

"What did he just say?" Ryan asked.

"He wants them to look through our bags."

One of the men grabbed her bag off her shoulder, unzipped it, then dumped its contents across the ground. A second man did the same thing with Ryan's bag.

"Any knives? Weapons?" Yuri asked her.

She pressed her lips together as the man searched the pockets, refusing to answer while at the same time hoping they didn't find the survival knife she'd packed in the bag. It was one of the last gifts her father had given her. But it was too late. The man slid out the knife and slipped it into his pocket. Thirty seconds later, they were finished.

"Pick up your stuff. Both of you." Yuri grabbed a Snickers bar from the pile beneath her feet and ripped off the wrapper before taking a bite. "We need to go."

Ellie studied the surrounding terrain as she shoved her things into her backpack. The small airstrip was surrounded by thick trees for as far as the eye could see. This Amazon rain forest was twice the size of India and made up of floodplains, savannas and rivers. Not exactly a place they could simply walk out of, even if they did find a way to escape. The doctor had told her that the airstrip where they landed was less than a mile from the river—north, she remembered—but the plan had been to catch a ride downstream to where Reynolds would be waiting for her. There was no sign of the guide the doctor had promised to send.

"Trust me, there's nowhere to go out here, unless you want to run into something even more deadly," Yuri said, seeming to read her mind. He laughed, then took another bite of the candy bar as she slung the pack over her shoulder. "Without a guide, there is no telling what you might encounter out here."

He was right. Where could they run? She glanced at Ryan and caught the concern in his eyes. He'd come to take her out of here, and she'd just walked them both into a trap.

Yuri slapped his leg. "Time to go."

They left the open terrain of the airstrip behind and

marched toward the jungle with Yuri in front of them and Pedro and the other man trailing a few feet behind. The thick canopy of trees enveloped them as they stepped into the heavily forested terrain. Large trees with thick vines soared toward the canopy that blocked part of the sunlight. A bird called out beside her. If she was right, they were moving south, away from the village and deeper into the jungle.

"You haven't told us what you wanted," Ryan said.

She glanced at Ryan, who'd just spoken out loud her own deep-seated fears. Because while this could be nothing more than a random kidnapping and ransom scenario they'd just stepped into, her gut told her this was no coincidence. Though she had no idea how, Arias's men could have found her in Rio and somehow managed to track her next move here.

"Like I said, I'm simply the middleman," Yuri said. "And like your glorified pilot said, whoever is willing to pay the most wins. Today, you just happen to be the prize."

"Why?" she asked.

"Let's just say you've made someone very unhappy. Poking into things you shouldn't."

"Like my father's murder," she said.

She'd been right. This had to be the work of Arias, though she still had no idea how they'd found her.

"Even I didn't ask as many questions as you when I took this job." Yuri sidestepped a vine that was lying across the uneven path they followed. "You will find out when we get there."

"So where are we going?" Ryan asked.

"To a camp not too far from here."

Ellie fought against the mounting fear. Arias was known for his brutality, for his seemingly unlimited resources…and for the people working for him—hired to do his dirty work.

A small branch snapped as she stepped on it. How could she have been so stupid? She'd known the heavy risks of coming here. Knew exactly what Arias and his men were capable of doing, especially knowing how far his reach was. They'd found her in Rio, and yet somehow she'd managed to convince herself that her plan was invincible. That flying here would be the linchpin that took down Arias.

Instead, she'd only managed to put more lives in danger.

She glanced at Ryan, guilt saturating her far deeper than the sunlight hitting the spongy jungle floor. At least they hadn't tied her and Ryan up as they marched between the armed men. But why would they need to? Yuri was right. There was nowhere to run. And even if they did, there were plenty of other dangers in the forest besides the men holding them at gunpoint. Spiders, snakes, poisonous dart frogs. A chill shot through her despite the humidity. And if they ended up in the water, there were things worse to encounter than piranhas. For starters, the razor-sharp teeth of the *cañero*, who moved in packs and had sharklike jaws. Not to mention malaria, yellow fever, dengue fever, that humidity made a breeding ground.

She tried to shut down her negative train of thought. Because it wasn't the wildlife threatening to kill them right now. Instead, it was three armed men. And while she'd clearly read too many travel blogs about the risks

of traveling in South America, no travel blog had told
her how to deal with this situation.

Ellie stumbled over a tangled vine crossing their
path. Ryan reached out to catch her arm with his hand.

"You okay?"

She glanced at where he was holding her and nodded. "Yeah."

The suffocating humidity pressed in against her
chest. "I'm sorry."

"Don't even go there. This isn't your fault. I agreed
to come."

"Something tells me if you had known things were
going to turn out this way you'd never have agreed to
come."

"I'm a saturation diver. I've never exactly gone out
of my way to avoid dangerous situations."

She filed his statement away as something to follow up on later. But not now. "When's the last time you
were marched through the Amazon jungle while being
held captive by armed men with a known cartel leader
wanting you dead?"

"I suppose you have a point." Ryan let out a low
chuckle. "If I had known all of that, I actually might
have avoided this."

"Options?" she asked.

"I'm not sure there are any right now."

"Shut up. Both of you."

She felt the jab of a rifle between her shoulder blades
from one of the men behind her as he shouted at them
in Portuguese.

She glanced at Ryan's tense jaw, knowing he was,
like her, searching for just that—options. Because while

she might have learned how to navigate Rio the past few months, this was an entirely different world. Her gaze lowered, then stopped at a string of large red welts on his arm. She had no idea what he'd gotten into, but he was clearly allergic to something. She had antibiotic cream in her bag, but there was nothing she could do to help him right now.

Someone shouted behind them.

Ellie stopped and turned around. Three armed men crashed through the jungle from their left, waving their weapons and shouting in Portuguese.

"Ellie…" Ryan pulled her behind him for protection. "Translate for me. What are they saying?"

"I don't know. They're upset about something."

The two groups of men shouted back and forth at each other in Portuguese, their guns aimed at each other in a showdown.

"What are they saying?" Ryan asked again.

"Something about money…stealing what is theirs."

She stumbled out of the way as one of the other men cracked his weapon across Pedro's head. She glanced around her. The forest spread out in all directions. Even if they did run, she had no idea where they were, but maybe that didn't matter. Maybe they needed to simply run.

One of the men fired their weapons. One of Yuri's men fell to the ground. Ellie stumbled backward to avoid getting knocked down as she watched the blood spread across his leg.

"Ryan…"

He grabbed her hand. "Run."

* * *

Ryan grabbed Ellie's hand and charged deeper into the jungle, praying the decision to run wasn't going to get them both shot.

"If they come after us—"

"Just keep running." He caught the panic in her voice, but if they slowed down—hesitated at all—they'd both be dead. And that wasn't the only thing he was concerned about. If they didn't escape now, his gut told him their odds of making it out alive were even slimmer. Because once their captors got out of them whatever it was they were after, they'd likely dump their bodies into the river. And if that happened, no one would ever find them.

The problem was, he had no idea which way to run except for away from the men who'd captured them. Adrenaline shot through him as they pressed down the untamed path away from the men whose shouts continued to echo through the thick canopy of the jungle. They'd been walking for at least twenty minutes before the other men had shown up. Maneuvering through the thick vegetation, though, was proving to be difficult. There was no trail. No clear route. Only skyward trees covered with vines that left him worried they would end up running in circles.

He could still hear the men shouting in the distance. Another weapon fired. He glanced back and caught shadows moving in their direction. They were coming after them now.

Sweat ran down Ryan's neck. If he was right, the runway was behind them, which meant they were probably moving farther away from the nearest town. But if he guessed wrong, they might never make it out. And with the density of the forest, civilization could be just beyond their line of sight and they would never know it.

He forced his mind to think as they ran through the brush. When they'd landed, he'd seen the river to the north, though he had no idea how close they were to the nearest town. It made sense to head toward the river. But even if they did find a town, he had no idea at this point who they could trust. From what he'd understood about the situation back there, Yuri and his men weren't the only people looking for them. Which didn't make sense.

Instead of continuing to search for answers that weren't there, he focused on the terrain, and getting them as far away from Yuri as possible through the dense forest. There were plenty of techniques he'd learned to use for low visibility when diving. He'd been in situations when clear water suddenly turned murky, dropping instantaneously from perfect visibility to less than a meter. Diving had taught him to stay calm, because panicking would only intensify the danger. The key was to take deep, regular breaths, slowly exhale and then consider your options.

But he had no gauges out here in the forest. No way to check air supply and depth. No exhaled bubbles to follow upward. Here they were surrounded by thick, wooded, marshy ground and tangled vines. There was nothing that would help with disorientation, or show them where the nearest way out was.

He squeezed Ellie's hand, noticing that she was struggling to keep up beside him. Because his job required working with heavy gear and equipment, he was used to intensive training with cardio and weights, and pushing his body's endurance, but even his heart was racing and his lungs burned from the exertion and the oppressive humidity.

"Ellie…"

She let go of his hand. "I need to stop. Just for a minute."

He started in a slow circle, searching the trees around them for movement while she worked—palms on her thighs—to catch her breath. He listened for the sounds of the men who'd come after them. The constant hum of insects was broken by the occasional bird and monkey. But there was no sign of any of the men. Had they actually gotten away?

"Do you have any idea which way we're going?" she asked.

"Not a clue. Do you remember how far the nearest village was from the airstrip?"

"According to the map, the village where we were supposed to go was the closest. About thirty minutes south of the airstrip. Dr. Reynolds had arranged for someone he knew to pick us up."

"Sounds like either his man didn't show up—"

"Or he saw what was happening and ran," she said. "And now everything looks the same. Trees, vines, water…"

She was right. There was no way to tell if they were headed toward a village. What he did know was that they were somewhere in the middle of a billion acres of rain forest full of rivers, piranhas, boa constrictors and jaguars. Not exactly easy to narrow down where they needed to go.

He felt a sharp sting bore into his arm, and he

brushed away the insect. "You ready? We need to keep going."

"I know, but you need some repellant. You've got welts up and down your arm, and they're not going to stop. I've got stuff in my backpack—"

"Later." He scratched his arm. "We need to keep going. It's just an allergic reaction, nothing seri—"

"Please." She dropped her backpack off her shoulder. "I need to fix something."

He grabbed her hands before she could unzip her backpack and pulled them toward his chest. "I know this is terrifying and I know you feel completely out of control, but we're going to find a way out of this. We need to keep moving."

She hesitated, then slid her pack back on. "I'm sorry. I just don't know how to fix this."

"For now, this will have to do." He quickly rolled down his sleeves as an attempt to stop the mosquitoes' feeding frenzy, glad he'd opted to wear long pants instead of shorts. Being eaten alive by these pesky insects was the last thing he needed.

He glanced behind him one last time as they continued pressing through the forest. He knew that if those men found them again, they weren't going to simply let them go. He was sure of that. What he didn't know was how long they'd be able to keep moving. Another ten minutes and they paused again. He held up his finger to his lips, signaling her to be quiet for a moment. The chatter of monkeys echoed around them, a bird called out, all of these sounds competing with the incessant drone of insects. There was still no sign of the men who'd been after them, but he wasn't ready to believe they'd actually lost them.

They continued moving at a steady pace, and Ryan was hyperaware of his surroundings. When he was a boy, he used to watch *National Geographic* specials with his grandfather and dreamed of exploring Africa's vast terrain. Instead, he'd ended up exploring the oceans. Today, he wished he had a machete, or something enabling him to hack away the thick brush. But he knew survival was never only physical. Being pushed to the limit mentally was where many people lost touch with reality.

"We've gone from racing across Rio on a motorcycle on our tail to this?" she said. "Any ideas on how to find our way out of here?"

"When we're lost underwater, we follow air bubbles to get to the surface. My best guess in this situation is that heading downhill should lead to water."

"And where there's water, there will be people." She glanced at him. "Anything would be better than staying in this jungle, though I guess you're not claustrophobic."

He could hear her labored breathing and the panic lacing her voice as they walked at a fast pace. "Can't be when you live up to twenty-eight days in a chamber under pressure doing back-to-back workdays of eight hours at a time. You finish work, shower and eat, then sleep because you're so exhausted."

"What's it like, working in an environment like that?"

"There are places with near zero visibility, where it feels as though you're surrounded by a heavy fog. But there are also locations that are clear all the way to the bottom." They skirted around a pile of vines. He was thankful for the diversion and had a feeling she was as well. "And while there's not a lot of time for sightseeing while on the job, there's the occasional peek at black coral, lionfish and other sea creatures."

Another ten minutes later they stumbled upon a wide stretch of river. Ryan stopped at the shoreline. A long canoe rested on the edge of the brown water, but beside that the forest simply stretched out around them. Acres and acres of trees, vines and water. Without a motor, if they attempted to go out in the boat, they'd be sitting ducks.

"A boat without a motor's too risky," he said.

"Agreed."

"I also think we need to keep moving down the shoreline. At some point, we'll run into people."

A howl echoed through the forest. Ryan turned away from the shore, searching for movement in the trees.

Ellie's face was flushed from the heat. It had to be getting close to three o'clock, and that meant the temperature was still fairly high. Without water, dehydration wouldn't take long to settle in. And the heat was already making them perspire, which was only going to speed up the dehydration process. On top of that, there was the constant threat of malaria and yellow fever from every mosquito that bit him. But they couldn't worry about that. Not when there were armed men after them. Because while heat stroke was a risk at this point, the odds of getting shot if the men found them again were probably even higher.

The brush rustled behind him. Closer this time. Ryan grabbed a thick stick off the ground, then turned to the right, ready to defend them. But his weapon wasn't enough. Ryan heard the click of a revolver. Yuri appeared a dozen feet away. Far enough that they could run, but close enough that it would be easy to take them down with a clear shot.

This time the man wasn't smiling. "Don't move, both of you, and put your hands in the air where I can see them."

FIVE

The camp the men led them to was nothing more than a couple of run-down buildings, where they'd apparently set up a temporary hideout in the jungle. Yuri had offered no information about the men who'd ambushed them or the man who'd gotten shot.

"I need your first-aid kit." Yuri grabbed her backpack, unzipped it, then dumped the contents onto the ground in front of them.

"What are you doing?" Ellie asked.

"One of my men was shot—"

"Wait." Ryan grabbed the man's hand. "This man needs medical help, not just a first-aid kit. There's got to be a clinic somewhere nearby."

Yuri pulled away. "I don't have a choice. The nearest clinic's an hour and a half from here by boat. We've got to stop the bleeding."

Ryan glanced at Ellie. "I've got some medical training. You've got to do this properly."

Yuri hesitated. "What are you going to do?"

Ellie stopped beside Ryan and studied the man who was lying on a mat on the ground in the shade of a large tree. While it was hard to feel sorry for him, blood had soaked through his leg. Avoiding infection in an environment like this wasn't going to be easy. Any bacteria from the bullet, the man's skin or clothing, or anything else that might have touched the wound could end up killing him. And if they could help, maybe their captors would end up being more sympathetic.

"I can flush the wound and cover it, but then you're going to have to get him to a doctor," Ryan said. "He's going to need antibiotics."

Ryan held the man's gaze while Yuri considered the offer.

"Okay, but don't try anything stupid."

"I can help," Ellie said.

Ryan nodded. "Good, because I'm going to need you. What do you have in your bag?"

"Just the basics. Antiseptic wipes, antibacterial ointment, bandages, medical tape, pain medicine."

"What about scissors?" he asked.

Ellie dug through the bag, then handed him a small pair.

The man groaned as Ryan cut away the clothing from the wound. "The good thing is that the bullet skimmed his thigh, leaving a narrow trench instead of a hole in his leg."

Ryan worked to flush out the wound with only an occasional instruction while Yuri continued hovering and Ellie tried to get the man to calm down. Five minutes later, Ryan covered the wound with a butterfly bandage Ellie had in her backpack, then gave the man some pills for the pain.

"We could help you get him to the nearest clinic," she said, catching Yuri's gaze.

"Forget it. If you think what you just did is going

to somehow buy your way out of here with your good deeds, it's not happening. The two of you aren't going anywhere."

Ryan grabbed a bottle of hand sanitizer and squirted the gel in his palm before handing it to Ellie. "How much are you being paid to keep us here?"

"Enough to make sure you don't escape again."

Yuri motioned to Pedro, who grabbed some twine and proceeded to tie them to two wooden chairs side by side at the edge of the clearing.

Ellie winced as the rope bit into her wrist. "Careful."

"I don't want to have a repeat of what just happened in the jungle," Yuri said, dumping their backpacks against the tree behind them. "We wouldn't want you to get lost again. There are dangers out there, so unless you know this place like I do, chances are you wouldn't make it out alive."

"That's so considerate of you," Ryan said sarcastically as the man walked away to check on the patient.

Ellie glanced at Ryan and caught the tension radiating up his jaw. Apparently, Yuri wasn't kidding as far as ensuring they didn't get away. She tugged on the rope behind her back. Unless they could manage to untie their bindings, he'd just nixed any chance of their escape.

Pedro came up to them, flipped around a third chair, then sat down in front of them. "I'm never sure what brings people like you to the Amazon. There's no cellphone service, no hot showers, no internet connections. None of the comforts of the big city. Just sticky humidity and giant mosquitoes everywhere."

While Yuri was the leader, Pedro was clearly the

muscle. Ellie tried to push down the waves of fear as she used her fingers to try to find the end of the twine. But the rope just bit into her flesh. The sun beat down on them while beads of sweat collected around the back of her neck. Right now, she wouldn't mind a few comforts from home.

"Then why do you stay here?" Ryan asked.

"For now, it pays for me to stay." Pedro leaned forward. "But I'm going to be the one asking the questions today. Starting with who were you meeting?"

"Would it be too hard to believe that we're just tourists on holiday?" Ryan clearly had no plans to play nice.

"That's not what your pilot told us. He told me you were planning to meet someone."

She glanced at Ryan. The only defense she knew was to call the man's bluff. "I never told the pilot anything. I simply hired him."

Which was true. But the question rattled her. If they didn't know who she had been planning to meet, at least they could be pretty certain that the doctor was okay. At least for now. But if they found out the real reason they'd come, they'd more than likely kill all of them. Including Dr. Reynolds.

"I've seen the contents of your backpack. Tourists bring suitcases with swimsuits, hiking clothes and cheap rain ponchos. Yours was packed for survival."

Ellie frowned. He clearly wasn't buying her answer.

"We're in the Amazon," she said. "I like to be prepared."

"Except I know who you are, Ellie Webb. I know your father was a judge who died in a house fire three months ago in the US."

"He was murdered."

"Ellie…"

She looked up at the sound of Ryan's voice, pulling away—for now—from that devastating moment.

"You know Arias?" Ellie's gaze shifted to Pedro's, her anger mounting. "Is this what he told you to do? Kidnap me? Because from what I've heard, he never does the dirty work. Instead, he relies on people like you to clean up his messes. And then, typically, they're the ones who end up taking the fall. Is that what you want?"

"Shut up, because remember I'm the one doing the questioning."

She'd been right about the hornet's nest. The wasps were beginning to swarm, and they'd ended up right in the middle of it.

"You can make this as hard or as easy as you want," Pedro continued. "So I'll ask you again. Who were you meeting here?"

Ryan still had a flicker of determination in his gaze. She never should have gotten him involved, but she also felt grateful he was here. She knew he'd do everything in his power to protect her. But there was no way to warn the doctor about what had happened. Which meant his life was in danger as well.

"Nothing?" Pedro let out a huff, then got up and grabbed a jar from a table a half a dozen feet away. He came back and squatted in front of them, then balanced the jar on Ryan's leg. Ellie stared at the dozens of large ants scrambling to get out of the jar. Something told her this wasn't going to end well if those ants got out.

"Do you know what these are?"

Neither of them answered.

"In your language they're called bullet ants," he said, answering his own question. "And while I've never been shot, I'm told that the sting of just one of these feels like a bullet ripping through your flesh. I was raised to be a warrior, and the test of the warrior is to challenge what this jungle offers. The pain of one ant will leave most people writhing on the ground in pain, and the pain can last for days. These ants have a toxin that interferes with a person's nervous system."

Ellie's mouth went dry. So this was it? They were going to be tortured for information in the middle of the Amazon jungle? And what happened if Ryan had an allergic reaction? There would be no one to help them.

Oh, God, please. Show us a way out of this. And please don't let people die for my choices.

"In my tribe," Pedro continued, "those who wish to become men and warriors will go through an initiation where we are stung by not just one but dozens of these ants without showing any signs of the pain. Here is what I find interesting, though. Your culture, on the other hand, has parties and eat and drink. It makes your people…soft. Which means it will probably only take one of these to get you to tell me what I want to know."

Pedro stood up and flashed her a smile as he walked toward her, then ran the smooth jar slowly down her cheek. She pulled away from his touch, sickened that someone would even consider torture.

"Leave her alone," Ryan said.

"I will. Once you've answered my question."

"Pedro…this isn't the time for this." Yuri walked up to them, the sun glistening on his brown skin.

Pedro frowned. "Just when I'm starting to have fun?"

"We need them alive and well, not rolling on the ground in pain. At least for now. Save those ants, though, because when Arias is done with them, I have a feeling he'll let you do what you want, but for now I need your help."

Pedro's frown deepened as he set the jar back on the table before the two of them walked away. Pedro was clearly irritated he hadn't had a chance to let the ants loose. And it was a reminder to her about what might still happen.

But at least they had a reprieve. For now.

Thank You, God.

"What are we supposed to do?" Ellie asked once the men were out of earshot.

"My opinion is while he might be right about the dangers of the jungle, I'd personally rather take my chances out there again."

"I agree," she said, despite the fact that the idea terrified her. "We have to leave."

"What about your wrists?" he asked.

"They've loosened some. I'm still working on them."

"Mine, too."

But was it crazy to make another attempt to escape? She glanced across the open camp, where the men were arguing about something. She kept working on the cords.

"There's a map in my backpack," she said. "I'm not sure how helpful it will be getting us through the jungle, but I've got water and a little bit of food.

"If we can make it back to the water, we can catch a ride to the next town," Ryan said. "But the first hurdle is getting loose and out of this compound."

She tugged again on the section of loose cord, which at the moment seemed impossibly tight.

The sun beat down on them. She watched a mosquito land on her arm and tried shaking her shoulder to shoo it away. Her back ached, and she was thirsty and hungry, but most of all she was terrified of what was going to happen next. The jar of ants sat on the table in front of them, a reminder that this was no game.

She glanced back at Ryan. One thing, though, seemed clear. If they didn't get out of here now, they weren't going to get out of here alive.

Ryan drew in a deep breath, then let it out slowly. His muscles ached and the swollen bites on his arms itched like fire. It wasn't the first time he'd had to deal with the hazards of a potentially deadly situation. Every day he went out on the job, he had to be willing to adapt. Had to expect something to go wrong. He spent his days working in the dark, most of the time with only a headlamp to light what he was doing. He'd run into bull sharks and wolf eels. The bottom line was that there was a small percentage of people actually able to hold up under the job's physical and psychological tolls of what he did on a day-to-day basis. And even though everyone on his team relied on each other, they couldn't guarantee that nothing would go wrong. But today felt different. He was responsible for someone else this time.

Ellie had come into this situation fighting for her life, which was part of why he couldn't blame her for the decisions she'd made. She'd seen her father murdered, and now they were after her. If the situation had been reversed, he'd have done exactly the same. And what choice did she really have? To possibly spend the rest of her life running, or face the enemy head-on? No, the choice was obvious, even though the outcome wasn't what either of them had expected.

But it wasn't over yet. He planned to go down fighting, and he knew she felt the same.

He opened his eyes and glanced across the compound to where Yuri was talking on a SAT phone. Apparently, there weren't many places left in the world where you couldn't make a call if you had the right equipment, including the Amazon rain forest. At the moment, they'd left them alone. But all that could change. How was he supposed to keep her safe when he had no way to take control of the situation? He should have listened to his father when he'd told him to take the next flight out of Brazil and persuade her to go with him. And yet was it really his place to make a decision like that? But neither could he have let her come here on her own. And from what he'd seen, there would have been no amount of arguing to change her mind.

"Are you okay?"

He turned to Ellie at her question. "Just thinking."

"About?"

"How to get out of here."

"You really think it's possible?"

"Let's just say I like the odds of leaving far more than the odds of staying."

"I know, but how are we supposed to leave?"

He studied her profile. Her breathing seemed labored and her skin had paled. "Ellie, take a slow, deep breath."

She bit the edge of her lip. "I'm sorry."

"You have nothing to be sorry about." Which was

true, but somehow, he needed to help her calm down. "Just…think of me as your diving buddy."

"Your diving buddy?"

"When you dive, the faster you breathe, the faster you will end up running out of air. One of the first things you learn is the need to conserve the oxygen in your tank."

"This is why I don't dive," she said.

"The first time I went diving, I panicked. All I could think about was escaping, except I was thirty feet underwater. We got caught in a current, and instead of focusing on what I'd been taught to do, my mind went blank. Thankfully my diving buddy got my attention. I was able to slow down my breathing, and I made it out of there without any complications."

"Every time I try to calm down I panic."

"Seriously, Ellie. You've been through a lot these past few months. Give yourself a break."

"I'm trying, but how do you deal with that on a daily basis when you're diving?"

He continued working on the cords as he mentally switched his mind back to his job. While he rarely volunteered information on what he did for a living, it always made for an interesting conversation when people found out.

"It depends on the assignment, but whether I'm laying out pipelines, or inspecting underwater structures, or just doing maintenance, I know I can't forget the risks. They are always in the back of my head. If I did, I'd probably get cocky and end up dead. You learn patience and focus, and it becomes more of a mental game than physical."

"And the other people you work with? Confined in such small quarters would have to bring out the worst in people. Or at least it would in me."

"There's always the occasional tough bloke that likes to stir things up. But honestly, when working in such a confined space, there's no place for arguments and fighting. After a while they become more like family than coworkers. We rely on each other. We have to, because our lives depend on it."

"And you actually live underwater for a month at a time?"

"Think of it more like living in the berth of a submarine. There's a crowded living space with a small sitting area where we can watch TV. Through another tube is the bathroom, sink and showerhead. After a while it becomes...normal."

"Normal?" She let out a soft laugh. "I'm not sure about that."

He could tell by the rise and fall of her chest that her breathing had slowed. She was starting to refocus again, which was essential. It was the only way they were going to find a way out of here alive. But despite her vulnerabilities, there was a strength about her he wasn't even sure she felt. But he'd noticed it, along with how she was willing to sacrifice herself for the sake of someone else.

"What about eating on your submarine?" she asked.

"Food is sent down through a tube and tends to taste bland. Carbonated beverages go flat, things like Rice Krispies that contain air bubbles go flat. And when the job's done, it's still not over. We have to decompress a day for every hundred feet."

"Sounds more like a nightmare to me, with no escape."

The frown on her face deepened as her gaze shifted to the other men. Pedro was hovering over the injured man and Yuri was still on the phone. A nightmare with no seeming escape was exactly what they'd just walked into.

"What's your favorite part?" she asked.

He felt one of the knots loosen. "There isn't a lot of downtime under the water, but every once in a while I'll snag a few minutes to walk on the seabed for some incredible sights."

"The scariest thing?"

"Sharks always up my blood pressure."

That made her smile. "Then what makes you keep going back?"

He tugged on one of the cords, trying to get it to slip. "I thought you were an artist, not a reporter."

"Sorry." Her gaze shifted across the compound. "I just need to keep my mind from thinking about what's really going on."

"I know I won't do the work forever, but it's never been about the money, even though it is good. It's challenging and I guess I'm stubborn enough to keep at it."

He didn't tell her the real reason he'd buried himself in his work the past two years. How Heather's death had pushed him to a place he'd never imagined going to. And while he'd finally come to terms with her death, he wasn't sure he was ready to stop.

He took in her determined profile. At least not unless he had a reason to stop running.

"I know your father asked you to come check on me, but why did you agree?" she asked.

Her question took him by surprise. "There was an

opening on my calendar. Besides, how could I resist coming to the rescue of a maiden in distress."

She let out a soft laugh. "I'm serious."

"I was actually getting ready to go diving when my father called."

"For work?"

"No. For pleasure this time."

"Wait a minute…you work as a diver, then dive during your time off?"

He wiggled his left hand. The binds were loosening. "Trust me, most of my friends think I'm a bit crazy to spend my time off in the water, but there's a huge difference between working beneath the surface of the sea and actually spending time in the water for pleasure. And those same friends have never visited Fernando de Noronha."

"I think I've heard of that."

"It's an uninhabited group of islands in the Atlantic near the northeast coast of Brazil. I spent the last month working off the Brazilian coast and decided this was my chance."

"And as much as the thought of diving terrifies me, I bet it's beautiful."

"You can't even imagine. You really should consider going out on the water one day."

"Are you volunteering to be my guide?"

He shot her a smile. "I suppose since I'm the one who is responsible for this phobia, I should be the one who helps end it. Just imagine visibility up to sixty meters in some areas. Spinner dolphins, angelfish, sea turtles and manta rays, all within reach of a pristine deserted beach…"

"So the real story is that I ruined your vacation, and managed to get you kidnapped by the cartel."

"Well, when you put it that way."

He glanced toward the edge of the compound, which led back into the forest. The sun would be setting in less than an hour. According to Yuri, whoever had paid him to grab them was arriving in the morning. Their window of escape was quickly shrinking.

"We're going to find a way out. Because I'm still planning to return one day. I was going to explore one of the shipwrecks I'd been itching to visit. The *Corveta Ipiranga V-17* went down in 1983 and now rests on the bottom of the rocky ocean floor, allowing advanced divers to explore the interior of the ship."

"That sounds...terrifying."

"Stop...because when we get out of this, I'm going to take you with me. Snorkeling for a day, then on a dive. You'll thank me for it."

"I think you're delirious." She leaned forward, intent on what she was doing.

"You okay?" he asked.

"Yeah. Where are they?"

"Looks like they're still dealing with their wounded comrade."

"Good." She turned her head and caught his gaze. "Because I'm free."

SIX

Ellie stared out across the open space to where their captors stood. "I'm free, but Pedro's watching, and we still need some kind of distraction."

"And we need it to be darker."

For the moment, Yuri still seemed focused on the man who'd been shot. And while she felt sorry for what had happened, she knew there was nothing more they could do to help. Taking him down the river to the clinic seemed like the best response, in her opinion. Emergency care wasn't easy to find in a place where the lack of medical resources meant people died from things that might have been treated with simple antibiotics. And her best guess was that Dr. Reynolds's clinic was well over an hour away.

Before long, darkness was going to settle across the surrounding jungle, which would help hide them if they escaped. But they'd tried to escape once before and that hadn't ended well. What was going to make this attempt any better?

The other issue was that these men knew this area, and she and Ryan didn't. Which put them at a serious disadvantage. They had no idea what they'd encounter or where they needed to go.

She kept her hands together behind her back in case they came back, not wanting them to notice she was free. They needed to make a decision. Their backpacks sat against a tree, six feet or so from them. They were another dozen feet from the edge of the jungle. They could grab their bags and run, but she still wasn't convinced they'd make it. How far could they get in the dark with no idea where they were going?

"What about your cords?" she asked.

"I'm getting there."

Ellie let out a huff of air. They'd notice if she tried to help him. Running through the jungle—traversing the uneven ground—was going to be difficult. He was going to need to have his hands free.

We need options, God.

She could smell fish frying at a fire near where Yuri and Pedro were drinking, which would slow down their reaction time. Her stomach grumbled. The last time she'd eaten had been hours ago. Yuri had warned them of the risks of running and probably assumed they weren't going to even try to escape.

"If we head north," Ryan said, nodding behind them, "we should hit the river. Yuri and his men have to have a boat to get in and out of here. We just have to find it, or a ride."

"How far do you think?"

"It's just a guess, but I'd say in calculating how long it took us to get here, three…maybe four miles."

"And you think we can do this in the dark?"

"We wouldn't be able to use it for a while, but you've got a flashlight in there, right?"

She nodded, grateful Yuri and his men hadn't taken it. But heading into the jungle scared her almost as much as having to swim in the open water. The jungle at night was going to bring its own set of issues. And the truth was, her fears held validity.

Mind still running, she shifted her gaze to the table. The ants.

"What about the ants as a distraction?"

If their kidnappers caught them running into the jungle—which she was certain they would—they'd come after them. But if they had something to slow them down, or even stop them, it could buy them the time they needed.

"That might work," Ryan said. "A hundred or so loose ants crawling on them…"

She shuddered at the thought, but it might just work. She glanced back at the men. They both had their backs to them for the moment.

She stood up. "I'm going to grab them now—"

"Ellie, wait…"

"They're not paying attention to us at the moment," she said, ignoring his warning. This could be their one chance.

She bridged the gap between her chair and the table, her heart pounding as she grabbed the jar, then headed back toward the chair. Seconds later she was back in the chair, grasping the jar of squirming ants behind her.

"I've just gotten loose," Ryan said.

"Then take the jar. You take care of the ants, and I'll grab the bags when we run."

And pray until then that their plan worked.

Their chance came sooner than she thought. A minute later, Pedro sauntered over to them with a bottle of liquor, stopping their conversation. "Not thinkin' of running, are you?"

He laughed, like the idea was ludicrous.

Ellie clasped her hands together behind her, praying he didn't decide to check and make sure she couldn't get loose. But thankfully, the thought didn't seem to have crossed his mind.

"I guess we've already learned that doesn't exactly seem like a good idea," Ryan said.

"Had a group of tourists a few months ago that decided to spend the day hiking without a guide. They had a map and their compass and a couple bottles of water."

Ellie looked away, not interested in playing the man's games.

"Authorities found them a week later. According to the news, one died of snakebite, and another from dehydration. Just remember that." He kneeled down in front of her and tilted up her chin with his thumb. "And by the way, we're making dinner later, if you're free."

He laughed again.

The smell of liquor permeated his breath. She pulled back from his touch, fear seeping through her. Her gaze shifted to Ryan. There were no other options. They needed to leave no matter what the risks.

The muscles in Ryan's jaw flinched. "Yuri told you to leave us alone."

"Yuri isn't in charge of me."

The man had been drinking too much, but she couldn't count on Yuri to defend her again. Ryan lunged toward him, taking Pedro by surprise. Pedro knocked Ryan onto the ground with the heel of his boot.

"Do you seriously think you can challenge me in your position?" Pedro asked.

Yuri ran across the yard at the commotion. Ryan grabbed the jar of ants, opened the lid, then flung the insects on the men.

"Ellie—run."

Adrenaline pumping through her, she felt her body switch to flight mode as she obeyed Ryan's order. She grabbed both packs and ran for the edge of the wooded jungle. She glanced back. Both men were already on the ground groaning.

Fear pushed her forward. In the lingering daylight, they needed to hurry. Once inside the forest, the heavy canopy filtered out most of the light. In another thirty minutes, heavy darkness would surround them. She needed the flashlight, but using it too soon meant a risk that the men would see them.

Ryan ran a couple of steps behind her. There was still no sign of the men, but she knew that eventually they'd start searching for them. A monkey howled in the distance, sending a chill down her spine with its haunting cry. She'd read about howler monkeys and their deafening calls that could be heard for miles. Maybe all of the animal noises would mask the sound of them crashing through the jungle.

She tried to erase the sense of déjà vu and instead focused on moving forward as fast as she could, not on the fact that the men would come after them.

"You okay?" Ryan asked.

"Yeah."

She glanced behind her, still unsure they were even going in the right direction. But Ryan had been right. If they made it to the river, they could find Yuri's boat and go downstream to the next town to get help. She slowed down to step over a rotten log. There was no true trail. Just the seemingly endless rain forest surrounding them.

She tried to swallow the waves of fear. Her lungs burned from the excursion. The humidity of the jungle pressed in around her. Mosquitoes buzzed everywhere. Forget about the dangers of this place—the only thing she cared about was leaving Yuri and his men as far behind as possible.

Fifteen minutes later the last of the light had almost faded, making it almost impossible to traverse the uneven jungle floor.

Ryan pressed his hand against her forearm. "We're going to need that flashlight now."

She paused. "Yes, but do you think it's safe to use it?"

"I don't think we have a choice. They might see us, but we'll never make it through this forest without some light."

Ellie dug around in one of the side pockets and pulled it out. She saw the insect repellent next to it and pulled it out as well.

"You're getting eaten alive."

"Better these annoying mosquitoes than one of those bullet ants."

She shivered despite the heavy heat as she sprayed him with the repellent. She was tired of running. Tired of looking over her shoulder everywhere she went. The nightmares of her father's death had slowly started to fade over the past few weeks, but not the constant fear of being caught.

"You're sure we're going the right way?" She flashed her light into the darkness. All she could see were trees and more trees.

"No, but I think so."

Neither of them could be certain. They started again at a slow jog, careful to avoid a fallen, rotting log. Shadows from the flashlight pooled around them, seeming to chase them through the darkness. The beam caught two eyes glaring in the underbrush. Ellie picked up her pace, ignoring the urge to panic.

Minutes passed between them in silence. She tried not to imagine what was out there beyond the light of her flashlight, and Ryan, she was certain, was working on a plan to get them out of this. At least there hadn't been any sign of their captors. But this was far from over. They were still miles from an airport, and there was no one at this point who could snatch them out of the jungle to safety.

Something caught her attention about fifty yards ahead of them.

"Ryan…" She stopped short, then shifted the angle of her flashlight. It caught the reflection of the water.

"Their boat has to be near here," he said as they made their way to the shoreline. Her feet were covered in mud and her stomach wouldn't stop grumbling, but she didn't care. They'd just found a way out.

Five minutes later, they found a long wooden boat with a motor moored along the shore.

"You okay with going out on the water?" he asked.

"Let's just say I've had to do a lot of things over

these past few months that I'm not okay with. But when your life depends on it, there aren't any other options than to press through, the impossible suddenly becomes possible."

Ryan helped Ellie climb into the boat and handed her both backpacks, then stepped into the back of the boat to check out the motor. Someone wasn't going to be happy when they discovered their transportation was missing come morning, but with no other options, all he could do was hope it found its way back to them. Unless it actually did belong to Yuri.

"I'm assuming you know how to start this thing," she said, shining the flashlight so he could see the motor.

He chuckled at her question. "Remember I make my living on the water. My grandfather and I used to go fishing in a boat pretty similar to this one, actually. Let's just hope it starts."

The original starter cord had been replaced with a shoestring. Talk about makeshift mechanics. He grabbed the end and pulled on the cord.

Nothing.

He gave it a second, then tried again.

Ellie glanced toward the shoreline. "Do you think it will run?"

"I don't know. Can you shine your flashlight over here?" She complied and he opened the fuel tank and checked the level. There was enough to get them to the next town at a minimum, plus a jerrican of fuel.

He tried pulling on the starter cord again. This time the motor caught.

"Looks like we're in business," he said, easing them away from the shore.

He studied the current. If they went downstream, it should feed into the main river. The boat slid through the black water lit only by the half-moon that hung to the east, giving him a sense of direction.

In the darkness, he couldn't read her expression, but he was pretty sure what she was thinking by the inflection of her voice. As much as he knew she wouldn't like it, his job right now was simply to get her out of here and to safety. She might not want to go back into hiding, but it was better than being dead. And if Yuri and his men found them, that was exactly what was going to happen. Which meant he was going to have to convince her to forget about the doctor and who had murdered her father for now and get her out of the Amazon.

Alive.

He followed the streaks of moonlight reflecting in the water. The shoreline was filled with gnarled trees and vines that spread into the water.

"I think I hear something."

Ryan let the motor idle at her statement. Noise of another motor rumbled behind them.

"Looks like another boat."

"If we could get their attention—"

"Ellie, wait."

He caught her frown. "What's wrong?"

"It sounds like a speedboat, but we don't know who's in it. Tourists are usually on riverboats, not speedboats. There are pirates out here on these waters."

"Pirates? You've got to be kidding me. As if I didn't

have enough to worry about, you're telling me it could be a pirate?"

"I just want to make sure we don't find help in the wrong place."

The second boat hummed in the distance as it got closer.

"I thought pirates were off the coast of East Africa and Somalia."

"I read a lot when I'm not working. One of the articles I read was about the growing issue of piracy along the Amazon. They strike riverboats and tourists, but they also go after locals who use boats and are just as vulnerable."

"What exactly are they after?"

"Fuel is one of their main targets, but from what I read, they'll take anything. Electronics, food, cash, watches, drug stashes—whatever they can get their hands on."

"And I just thought I had to worry about piranhas and electric eels. And the authorities? What are they doing?"

"Sounds like it's more of a losing battle. We're talking about a place almost the size of the US, and these pirates know the terrain, more than likely better than those trying to track them down."

Ryan cut the motor and let the boat float toward the shore into the shadows, away from the moonlight, using the oars to guide them. A bright beam of light swept past them in the water, as if they were looking for something. For them? Ryan shoved away the thought. It wasn't possible. Or was it?

"Get down," he ordered.

He laid down next to her on the bottom of the boat

as it bobbed in the water next to the shoreline. If they stayed still, hopefully they would look like nothing more than an empty boat, waiting for its owner to return in the morning. White light swept across the trees behind them. Water lapped against their boat. His arms wrapped around her shoulders. Voices from the other boat carried across the water.

If they'd found them...

The bright light swept the water just beyond them, then cut away as they passed them and headed slowly downstream. Ryan let out a whoosh of air and realized he'd been holding his breath.

He took a chance and looked out over the edge of the boat. The other vessel was only a shadow and disappeared into the darkness downstream.

"I think we've lost them, but we need to keep going."

"Do you think they were looking for us?"

"I don't know. It could be Yuri...could be pirates... could be anyone."

If they encountered them again, there was no way they could outrun a speedboat. Heading back into the jungle seemed just as futile. Which left them—once again—out of any viable options.

Ryan hesitated. The sound of the motor began to grow louder as the boat turned around and headed back toward them. They'd seen something. A light flashed, reflecting off the boat.

"Ellie, stay down."

Seconds later, a shot fired, hitting the water a few feet from their boat.

Whoever was out there had just found them.

SEVEN

Ellie dived back into the bottom of the boat as another shot rang out. She couldn't tell where it hit this time, but it had to be close. Someone shouted at them in Portuguese to surrender. Her heart quickened. There wasn't time to panic. Wasn't even time to think through what they needed to do.

"Stay down." Ryan scrambled toward the motor. "We've got to get out of here."

Ellie struggled to catch her breath. She knew that the wooden boat they were in couldn't protect them from a bullet. Even from the bottom of the boat she could see the lights from the other vessel reflecting against the trees behind them. The pursuing boat was heading back toward them and it was just a matter of seconds before they overcame them.

The beam of light reflected off Ryan. He pulled on the motor cord. Nothing. If the cord broke or he didn't get it going, they were nothing more than sitting ducks. Though even if they could get the boat started, she wasn't sure they'd actually be able to outrun the other boat.

Let it start, let it start...please, God.

A second later the motor started. Ryan swung the

boat around and sped upriver. They were going in the opposite direction from the town. Now they were going deeper into the Amazon. She had no idea what lay ahead on the banks of the river, or even how far it was until the next town. But whatever sat in the shadows beyond the shoreline couldn't be worse than what they were facing right now.

Gripping the edges of the boat, Ellie searched the river for an escape while water sprayed against her face. She knew enough about the river to realize there were dozens of tributaries and waterways that wound their way through the vast rain forest, but trying to lose their pursuers was more than likely going to be futile. Like with Yuri and the jungle, she had no doubt that whoever was behind them knew these waterways inside and out. She and Ryan didn't.

In the darkness, the water surrounding them looked like a sea of black ink, marred only by a trail of white light from the moon and the occasional flash of light from the other boat. She had no idea how deep the water was or what lay beneath the surface. And neither did she really want to know. A shiver sliced through her as she crouched deeper in the bottom of the boat, then glanced behind them. From her vantage point, she could see the lights of the speedboat coming toward them.

Warm wind rushed past them as Ryan raced upstream, but while the boat they'd confiscated might be great for fishing, it clearly wasn't good for speed.

"Won't it go any faster?" she shouted above the roar of the engine while continuing to watch the pursuing boat.

"I can't. I'm pushing the motor as it is."

Moonlight bathed the tips of the trees in its white

light, then spilled onto the water. Her gaze searched the shadows ahead of them now for a way out. Something caught her eye a few dozen yards ahead of them. A split in the river with a narrow tributary heading off to the right. She prayed as they sped through the water, the wake spraying droplets against her face. A game of cat and mouse with pirates or the cartel wasn't going to end well if they got caught.

"Ryan…" Ellie leaned forward from the front of the boat. "Look up ahead."

"I see it."

At the Y, he steered the boat sharply to the right and followed the shadows into the narrow tributary as fast as the vessel could go. The moon had gone behind a cloud, cloaking them—for the moment—in darkness. Ellie glanced behind them. There was no sign of the light from the other boat. Ryan pressed on for another mile, then cut the motor to a slow idle and let the boat drift toward the shoreline, hoping the sound of the other boat's motor canceled out the sound of their own. He let it glide beneath a wide swath of tree limbs, with just enough space for the boat to hide beneath its cover. An eerie silence hung around them, broken only by the constant buzz of insects and an occasional call of a monkey. But no sound of the speedboat that had been pursuing them.

She glanced back at Ryan, who was nothing more than a silhouette as the boat bobbed near the shoreline. Ellie prayed that the other boat would give up their search, prayed that the shadows and trees along the shoreline would hide them if they followed.

"You think we lost them?" she asked, keeping her voice to a whisper.

"I hope so, but it's impossible to know."

Her gut told her that if they didn't find them right away, they would continue searching. But how long would they keep searching until they gave up?

The boat rocked beneath them. If these were simply pirates looking for valuables, they were going to be disappointed. Neither of them had anything of value other than the clothes on their backs and some worthless things in their backpacks. But if it was Yuri and his men who were chasing them, then it wasn't their stuff they were after. And that was what scared her.

"If we can get to the nearest town and find transport to Manaus," Ryan said, "my father can arrange private transport for us out of the country."

Ellie glanced back at Ryan. She should have listened to him and his father from the beginning. But now it was too late. A light reflected on the water in the distance. They must have come back and decided to search the tributary. Ellie's breath caught as the light came toward them. "I don't think we can outrun them," Ryan said, "but if we stay hidden, we might have a chance."

Ryan started the engine again. Ellie held on to the sides of the boat, holding her breath as he maneuvered farther into the thick brush, then cut the motor again. The boat continued to bob beneath them. Ellie drew in a breath, keeping her gaze focused downriver.

She closed her eyes for a moment. When she'd lain in bed back in Rio, listening to every sound in her apartment, one of the places she'd gone to in her mind was back to those summers spent in Colorado. Ryan had been part of most of those summers, though she hadn't thought about him in years. Not really. He'd simply been an annoying boy.

But today, all of that had changed.

She glanced at Ryan. It seemed ironic he was the one who'd arrived to help rescue her. Never in a million years would she have predicted that one day she'd put her life in his hands and in turn trust him completely. But that was exactly where she was.

The spotlight from the speedboat hit the trees above them, yanking her back to the present. She could see the movement on the water through the trees as the other boat slowed down a few dozen yards from them. She drew in a lungful of air and held it as the vessel crept past them, searching the shoreline with their light. The humid air pressed in around her. A mosquito buzzed in her ear. All they needed was a few more seconds.

She found herself counting off the seconds. One, two, three… The boat was past them now. Four, five, six…

Keep going, keep going…

The boat stopped upstream from them. Ellie blew out the breath she'd been holding. Their light searched the trees on the other side of the tributary. Someone shouted, but she couldn't understand what they were saying. They swung the light to the other side of the boat and into the trees in front of them. A moment later the light hit Ryan's chest.

Her stomach dropped. They'd found them.

The men's shouts carried across the water.

Another bullet fired, this time hitting the side of the boat. Water started seeping into the bottom of the craft.

"Ryan, we've been hit."

The only escape at this point was the shoreline, but it was still a dozen feet away through the swampy water. Another wave of panic broadsided her. Even if it was possible to get to the shore, it didn't matter. It was already too late.

The boat had maneuvered in behind them, shining a light on them and aiming their weapons at them.

A man she didn't recognize shouted something in Portuguese, then switched to English. "Put your hands up where I can see them."

He shouted more orders at the other men. Water was now rapidly filling the bottom of the boat. In another minute, it would sink. Ellie moved next to Ryan, then held up her hands. How had it come to this? Being rescued by the very men who had been out looking for them. She glanced at the shoreline and then back to Ryan, desperate for another way out, but there wasn't one.

One of the men stepped down into their boat, grabbed her and forced her onto the other boat.

"What do you want?" She could hear the tone of her own voice, was surprised at how calm she sounded. Because inside she felt anything but calm as the reality of what was happening began to sink in. The past twelve hours had become nothing more than one long nightmare that wouldn't end. But this time she knew she wasn't going to wake up back in her bed in Rio.

She stumbled onto the deck of the boat, next to Ryan. They stood in front of four men who each carried a sidearm. The leader had lighter skin with a slim build.

"What are they saying?" Ryan asked.

"I don't know. They're not speaking Portuguese anymore."

"What do you want?" Ryan took a step forward.

"Give me your backpacks," one of them shouted.

Fingers trembling, Ellie undid the latch and handed someone her bag for the second time. "There's nothing of value in there."

The man frowned and dumped out the contents, clearly disappointed. "It doesn't matter."

"Then what do you want?" Ryan repeated. "Let us go."

They were heading away from the shore now. She grabbed on to the rusty railing to catch her balance as the boat picked up speed and headed back toward the main artery of the river.

"Sit down. Both of you."

One of the men grabbed her arm and led her across the deck before shoving her onto a bench at the back of the boat. At least they hadn't tied them up yet. Not that there was anywhere to go. Or anywhere to find help.

The leader stood in front of them with a smirk on his lips. "I don't need you to have anything of value."

"What do you mean?" Ellie asked.

The man shot them a toothless grin, held up his cell phone and showed her a photo as the boat flew down the river. "There's a price on your head."

Ellie's stomach soured as she stared at the photo that had been used on news channels three months ago announcing her death. A chill shot through her as the man confirmed that their capture hadn't been simply another random tourist kidnapping. It had always been about finding her. Which meant they were back where they started. With no idea where they were. No idea where the nearest town was. If there was a bounty on her head, then nowhere was safe.

Ryan waited to talk with Ellie until the men headed toward the other side of the boat. "We need to get off this boat. Now."

"How in the world are we supposed to do that?" He caught her confused expression. "There's four of them and they're armed."

"If we wait, they're going to turn us over to Arias's men. And we know what will happen then."

"Do you have a plan?"

He glanced out across the white trail of churning water behind them, then toward the dark shoreline, knowing she wasn't going to like his answer. "We jump."

Her eyes widened. "You're kidding, right? There's no way I'm jumping into the water."

"I'm very serious."

"I can't, Ryan—"

"If we don't, we'll end up exactly where we were a few hours ago. And at least at this point we're not tied up. But if we wait, and they decide to tie us up, our options will vanish."

Which was going to be a death sentence. He felt certain about that. But how was he supposed to convince her that jumping into the water was their only way out of this?

He caught the fear in her eyes as she glanced at the frothy water churning behind them. The water beyond the lights of the boat was as black as the sky above them.

"You're a diver, so this might sound ridiculous to you, but I have this irrational fear of water. All I can think about is that if I jump," she said, "I'll probably break my neck. And if that doesn't happen, there are always the piranhas. I'm not liking the way this is going to end no matter what we decide to do."

"First of all, piranhas don't typically eat people—"

"Maybe not, but I'm pretty sure there's something in there that would be happy to eat me for dinner."

"Think about it, Ellie. They're not expecting us to jump. It's the only advantage we have, and this might be the only time we have."

Lightning flashed in the sky in front of them, catching the yellow eyes of what probably was a caiman in the water. Her chest heaved and her breaths became more rapid. She was in a full-blown panic attack.

"I can't do it, Ryan."

He took her hand. "Yes, you can."

She pressed her lips together. "That day I jumped into the pool to impress you... I couldn't breathe. And as childish as it seems, I knew I was going to die. If we jump into that water, we're going to die."

"If we don't jump into that water, we're going to die."

She still didn't look convinced. "But down there, in the dark... This isn't just my fear of water. We're in the middle of the Amazon, on the Amazon River in a boat run by pirates. You think they're just going to not notice? Not come after us?"

"What about if we don't? What happens then? These guys are going to take us back to Yuri and his men, or I don't know, maybe straight to Arias himself. He'll find a way to get the information he wants out of us—in a way that will probably make bullet ants look tame— and then that's it. They won't let us go." He squeezed her hand. "I know you can do this. For the past few months you've proved just how strong you are. You've lived on the run with the cartel after you, and you survived. Getting in this water and swimming to shore, that's going to be a piece of cake compared to everything you've been through."

The men were still shouting about something toward the front of the boat. He knew he was right, but he also knew she was terrified. If they tied them up, though, they didn't have a chance. Jumping, on the other hand, might sound terrifying, but it was their only chance.

"And once we make it to shore?" she asked. "Then what? We're back in the jungle again. It's like a bad dream, replaying over and over."

"At least we'll be away from the men after us."

"There's a bounty on my head, Ryan. So we play another round of cat and mouse. You don't think they'll come after us again? Find us again?"

"I don't know what other option we have."

"I know. I just…"

"You're stronger than you think, Ellie."

She blew out a huff of air. "So what's your plan?"

"They're not paying attention to us for the moment, so we jump and make it to the shoreline. Hopefully, they won't notice right away that we're gone. Once we get to the shore, we run."

"What about our bags? I've got a waterproof waist pack, but the rest—it will just drag us down."

"Agreed. We can pull out the essentials. Our passports, the flashlight…"

She looked up at him, her eyes wide with fear, but also a sense of courage he'd noticed before. Emotion washed through him—something he couldn't quite identify. Not just a desire to protect her, but more than that. For the first time since Heather's death, he felt something that left him wishing they were somewhere else—anywhere else—so he could get to know her better.

He slammed shut the thought. Now was not the time. For the moment, he needed to stay focused on getting them out of here. Alive.

He glanced back at the front of the boat. The men still weren't paying attention to them. No doubt, it hadn't even crossed their minds that their captives were considering literally jumping ship.

"We'll try to slip into the water as quietly as we can. Then as soon as we hit the water, try to orient yourself and not panic, but don't worry, I'll be right there with you."

She still didn't look convinced. "Won't we skip or roll or…break something."

"I figure they're going about thirty miles an hour. Don't let go of my hand. And even if we do manage to get separated, I'll find you. I promise. We'll head to the shore. By the time we're off the boat, they'll be way ahead of us, which will give us time to get to the shore. And once we're there, we run."

"Again."

Being wet in the jungle with no supplies wasn't exactly his first option. But if they were going to get out of here alive, there was no choice.

"Ellie…"

He glanced back at the men. One of them was on a phone, probably one they'd stolen from a victim. Two of them laughed over something. No one was paying attention to them. But he worried they would stop soon, and if they did, it would be too late. They were running out of time.

"You can do this. We need to go. Now."

Five seconds later, she was stuffing their passports into her waterproof bag, which she then gave to him to strap around his waist. He grabbed her hand, took a deep breath and fell into the black waters surrounding them.

EIGHT

Ellie sucked in a lungful of air before her body hit the water. Immediately, the darkness of the river enveloped her. She tried not to panic as they plunged beneath the surface, but suddenly she couldn't hear anything. Couldn't see anything. Her only lifeline was Ryan's hand gripping hers as they frantically tried to get away from the pirates' boat.

Stay calm, Ellie. All you have to do is stay calm and get back to the surface.

The current was pulling them downstream, but no matter how terrified she felt, she couldn't panic. Couldn't let her thoughts wander to what was under the water now with them. Something knocked into her leg. Her body twisted away from it, ripping her hand loose from Ryan's. Terror engulfed her. She opened her eyes, still disoriented by the darkness. Ryan, her only escape, was gone.

Her arms flailed in front of her as her body shifted away from the object. Something bumped into her again. Was it Ryan next to her or something else? She couldn't tell. She needed to reach the surface, but she had no idea which way was up. Her lungs burned, her heart pounded, while fatigue swept through her limbs. Falling overboard wasn't what was going to kill her. It was not making it to the surface. That was how people died.

Or being eaten by some carnivorous fish.

She ignored the thought. Where was Ryan?

For a split second, she was fourteen again. Jumping off the roof, then slapping hard against the water of the pool next to Ryan's house. The water had sucked her under, leaving her unable to find the surface. Fear had flooded through her, making her mind freeze. In that moment—as foolish at it sounded—she'd been certain she was going to drown. And if she didn't find her way to the surface of the river tonight...

Something brushed against her leg again, but this time she ignored the sensation. Seconds ticked by. Her eyes burned in the murky water as she searched for light at the surface. What had Ryan told her? Follow air bubbles to get to the surface. She opened her eyes again and forced her mind to calm. Something grabbed her arm, but this time it was Ryan, holding her hand again and pulling her with him. She took in a lungful of the humid air at the surface and felt the panic start to dissipate.

"We're going to have to swim now," he said, pulling her toward the dark, forested shoreline.

Moonlight hit the dark swirls of water around them, as she worked to keep up with him, but there was no time to think about what they'd just done. Jumping off a pirate ship into the Amazon River had only been part of the plan. Which was why she couldn't let the situation paralyze her. Instead, she headed toward the shoreline beside him, kicking her legs and struggling to breathe in the precious air between strokes.

But where were the men who'd grabbed them? Had they discovered they were gone yet?

By the time they made it to the shore, the question was answered. She could hear the men shouting from their boat in the distance as they turned around and headed back up the river toward where they'd jumped off. The lights from the boat searched the water and the shoreline, but she and Ryan had already slipped into the darkness of the rain forest. She stumbled over a twisted vine as she struggled to orient herself to the new terrain. For someone who spent most of her days at her art desk—and worked out four or five days a week in the comfort of her local gym—the past few hours had stretched her physically. But at the moment it was fear and adrenaline that propelled her forward and gave her the edge she needed to keep up.

Her legs began to burn as she scrambled across the jungle floor beside Ryan. Water dripped into her eyes and ran off her chin, making her shiver despite the humidity. And even though she was out of the water, her lungs felt as if they were going to explode. She wasn't sure how much longer she could run, but neither would she let the all-encompassing fear let her stop. Flickers of white light from the boat shimmered periodically against the trees behind them as the men searched the water and the shoreline, edging closer to where they were.

A beam of light hit the trees above them.

Ryan pulled her behind a thick tree, motioning for her to be quiet. She pressed her back against the tree, heart pounding, breathing labored. He leaned into her, as they waited for the boat to move downriver.

A minute later, he took her hand. "They're gone. We need to go."

They started running again, down a rambling path, making her wish she had her flashlight. But the risk was too great.

"Do you think they'll be able to figure out where we hit the shore?" she asked, her voice barely above a whisper.

"I don't think so, but in case they do pick up our trail, we've got to keep moving."

The eerie sounds of the jungle along with the constant swarm of mosquitoes pressed in around her as she stayed close to Ryan. Glancing back, she didn't see the light from the river anymore, but there was still no way to know where the men were now, or if they'd stayed on the boat or decided to try to follow them into the night. But where were they supposed to escape to?

Five minutes later, she reached out for Ryan's arm, signaling him to stop again. She pressed her hands against her thighs and fought to fill her lungs with air. Right now, all she wanted was to crash and sleep.

But that wasn't going to happen. Not tonight anyway.

Despite the warm air, she was shivering. Her clothes were still wet.

Ryan stopped in front of her and brushed back a strand of her wet hair from her cheek. "Take a moment to catch your breath, but we need to keep going."

She nodded, even though he probably couldn't see. "I know."

I need Your strength, God. I don't know how much longer I can do this.

Because it wasn't just this moment that had her nerves about to snap. Weeks of hiding, sleepless nights listening for sounds that they'd found her. It had left her vulnerable and anxious. Was she ever going to be able to put this behind her again and find normal? Settle down with a decent guy like Ryan, have a couple kids and live happily ever after?

Or maybe there wasn't going to be normal again for her. Maybe this was going to be her new life.

Pushing away her rambling thoughts, the two of them started walking again, slipping through the darkness, surrounded by the constant buzz of insects. Lightning flashed in the sky, closer this time. The storm was heading their way, and from the look of the sky in the distance, rain was on its way as well. Ten minutes later, they came across an opening in the jungle. Ellie searched the tree line for signs of a village as thunder crashed above them and the first drops of rain began to fall. If they were going to get out of here, they needed to find someone—anyone—who could help. But they had no idea whom they could trust.

"Which way?" she asked.

"I have no idea, and I don't think your map would work even if we did have it."

Forget the map, she wished she had her phone, but that wouldn't work here, either.

"I think we've lost the pirates, so we need to follow the river. That's where we'll find people."

She nodded as shadows emerged into the clearing.

The sound of a gun being cocked made her rip her gaze toward the right.

"*Por favor*—please…" She held up her hands automatically, praying they hadn't once again run into the enemy.

Ryan grasped Ellie's arm as she continued speaking to the man in Portuguese. He looked to be in his late teens, maybe early twenties. If it wasn't for the weapon he held, Ryan would have considered trying to take down the man, but it wasn't worth the chance of either of them getting shot.

"What's he saying?" Ryan asked her.

"I told him we were grabbed by pirates. He says he knows those men. Last month they robbed him while he was out on his boat. He says they have brought fear to those who live along the water's edge. Fear to go out at night. Fear to do anything."

"I speak English." The man took a step forward, then held down his gun so it wasn't pointing at them. "My name is Diego."

Ellie quickly introduced herself and Ryan.

"I can help. I can take you to my village. You should be safe there."

"We don't want to endanger you or the lives of your family." Ellie glanced at Ryan, wondering, he was sure, how much they should tell him. "But we need to get to Manaus."

"I can take you there myself in my boat in the morning."

Ryan glanced at Ellie's face, lit up for a moment by the lightning flashing overhead. There was no way to know if they could trust him or if this was another trap.

If the man worked with the pirates or Yuri, they were going to end up right back where they had been.

"Why are you offering to help us?" he asked.

"Because I know who you are. I have heard rumors that there is a reward being offered for two foreigners," he continued. "But you must understand that not everyone is willing to sell their souls for a handful of money."

The man's words managed to put Ryan's concerns partially to rest. If what the man said was true, that he saw the pirates as the enemy, then that gave him motivation to help them. How much would it take for someone to be willing to turn away from their own set of ethics? The price on their heads had to be enticing. But he wasn't sure they had any choice but to trust him. They were both tired, hungry and wet, and they wouldn't survive long in the jungle on their own.

"What I said was true," Diego continued. "The men out there, we call them water rats. Because not only do they take things from tourists, they steal from their own people. That is why I am willing to help you."

"How far to your village?"

"Not far. Ten, maybe fifteen minutes."

Diego started walking in the opposite direction from the river and from where the pirates were searching for them.

"You said you'd encountered these pirates," Ellie said, hurrying to catch up with him. "What exactly happened?"

"I was out in my canoe fishing like I do every day. They tied me up, stole my GPS and my cell phone. I was terrified they would kill me."

"What about the authorities?" Ryan asked as the rain

picked up, though the canopy of trees above them blocked some of the downpour. "Aren't they doing anything?"

"They try, but catching them isn't easy. There is so much land and not enough people patrolling the river. These river bandits know this and take advantage of the situation. Some of them are even willing to take money to look the other way."

Ryan frowned. He'd seen his own share of corruption in his line of work. In third-world countries where the oil industry was run by a network of warlords, businessmen and corrupt officials. In the end, the money itself was never seen by the people who needed it most.

"Not too long ago, five masked pirates, all armed, boarded a fuel ship and stole three thousand gallons of diesel," Diego continued. "They also took the crew's cash, watches and other valuables. They rob passenger ships and boats filled with cocaine. And the police rarely come into these waterways. When they do, the pirates know the river well enough to escape. It is a battle difficult—if not impossible—to win."

Ryan slapped at a mosquito, one of hundreds, it seemed, that were buzzing around his head. He'd probably end up catching some tropical disease before this was over, but there wasn't exactly anything he could do about the fact that his body seemed to be turning into one huge, itchy red welt. And at the moment, there were more pressing issues to deal with.

Ten minutes later, a small settlement appeared. It was designed in a circle, made up primarily of what looked like bamboo houses. He glanced around at the simple layout, lit only by a couple lanterns. More than likely there was no electricity or running water, but he hoped there would be someone who had a cell phone they could use.

Diego called out to someone inside a house. A moment later a woman in a colorful shirt and skirt appeared.

"This is my mother." Diego quickly made introductions, then turned to the older woman. "She doesn't speak English, but I've asked her to fix you something to eat."

Within minutes, they were sitting at a rickety wooden table, and Diego's mother was hovering over the table that was now filled with fish, bananas and boiled manioc. For the first time in hours, he realized just how hungry he was.

"This is delicious," Ellie said, then started talking to the woman in Portuguese. The woman's face lit up as they chatted.

"I told her what happened to you," Diego said to Ryan. "Like me, she would do anything to help stop the men causing such panic on our river. Especially someone who threatened her little boy. She still calls me that."

"Your English is good, Diego." Ellie picked at a piece of fish while his mother left for the kitchen. "Where did you go to school?"

"Not here. Our village is too small to have a high school. We don't even have electricity." He shrugged his shoulders like it wasn't a big deal. "We would go in my boat two hours upriver to the nearest school."

"What was it like?"

"There are no books or desks, but students copy off the board and memorize their work. Now there is a teacher in Manaus who teaches us. We watch her lessons on a TV that we power by generators."

"I'm impressed," Ryan said. "What about furthering your education? There are schools in the cities you could go to."

"I've thought about leaving for the city, but then who would take care of my mother and my siblings? So for now, I stay. And maybe one day, I will become a teacher."

Ryan shifted in his seat, his own problems suddenly shoved into perspective. He'd dealt with loss, but not the never-ending need to source the basics like food and clean water. On top of that was the lack of medical care, schooling options and many things he took for granted, like running water and electricity.

Ellie slipped into the kitchen area to help Diego's mom clean up.

"Come," Diego said. "We can sit outside and watch the storm move past."

Ryan took his last bite of fish, then moved onto the veranda as the sky lit up.

"Is she your girlfriend?" Diego asked, leaning against the wooden railing.

"Ellie? No. I've known her since we were both kids. My father sent me here to help her. Then we ran into some trouble."

"She is pretty."

Ryan couldn't help but chuckle. "Yes, she is."

He glanced at the open doorway. He could hear Ellie chatting in Portuguese, while Diego asked him a question about soccer. Ryan struggled to focus on their conversation. Ellie *was* pretty…beautiful, in fact. And he certainly hadn't expected the strong feelings of attraction toward her. Not that any of that mattered. All he needed to focus on at this point was getting her safely out of the country.

A few minutes later, Ellie stepped out onto the veranda, stopping their conversation. "The rain has stopped. Diego's mother offered their hammocks for us to sleep in tonight."

"And in the morning, I can take you up the river," Diego said.

Ryan nodded. All they could do now was pray that no one looking for them found them in the meantime. He slapped at a mosquito, feeling as if they were slowly going to drive him insane.

"They like you," Diego said. "The mosquitoes."

"Too much," Ryan said.

"I have something that will help." Diego stepped off the porch, dug around in the dirt a little bit, then came back with dozens of tiny ants swarming on his hand.

More ants? Ryan frowned.

"Wait a minute. Do those bite?"

"They won't bite." Diego started crushing the ants on his arms and rubbing them across his skin. "You can smell this?"

Ryan leaned forward and hesitantly sniffed. "I can, but this is supposed to keep away the mosquitoes?"

"Try it."

Ellie sat down on one of the hammocks, swinging slowly back and forth with an amused grin on her face.

"You think this is funny?" he asked as he went ahead and smashed some of the ants across his arms.

"Very amusing," she said. "Though I think I should try it as well."

"You must trust me," Diego said. "You will notice the mosquitoes will leave you alone now."

"Thank you, Diego." Ellie finished rubbing the ants across her arms. "For everything. You and your family."

"The men who took you don't represent who we are. I want you to know that." Diego brushed off the rest of the ants from his arms. "In the morning, I will take you up the river in my boat to Manaus, where you can get help. But in the meantime, you must both sleep."

Ryan nodded, then glanced at Ellie. He just prayed he'd be able to keep her safe until then.

NINE

Ellie turned over so she could watch the stars through a crack in the tree line from her hammock. The storm had passed, leaving behind a trail of diamond-studded black sky. It reminded her of camping trips at Yosemite with her father. Hiking up to Glacier Point, with its incredible views of the valley and equally incredible views of the night sky. They'd gone every summer while she was still in high school and as often as they could despite their busy work schedules.

But now all of that had changed.

"Can't sleep?" Ryan's voice interrupted her thoughts from across the veranda.

"I'm exhausted, but the adrenaline's still pumping and my mind won't stop running." She sat up, swung her feet around and planted them on the wooden floor. A moonbeam left a trace of light across his face from his hammock, illuminating his strong jawline. She'd never expected Ryan to become her anchor in the storm, but somehow that was exactly what he'd become.

"I understand."

"I just can't stop thinking about everything. My father. My aunt. Dr. Reynolds. I'm worried Yuri or the pirates might have found him. I know we need to leave, but what about the doctor? What if he's in trouble?"

"Even after all that's happened?" Ryan asked, sitting up.

She let the hammock rock slowly beneath her. "I know. It's crazy, but I just can't stop worrying."

"Anything else bothering you?"

She struggled to put her emotions into words. "Sometimes—sometimes I miss my dad so much, it physically hurts. I keep thinking that all of this has to be some big mistake. That all I need to do is just wake up, and I'll be sitting back in his house, watching football or cooking burgers on his grill. Except that's never going to happen."

He sat quietly, waiting, she presumed, for her to continue.

"So much has changed. Three months ago, I was negotiating usage rights for some of my artwork with a client, and today…I'm fighting for my life. Sometimes I don't even know how I got here. All my friends think I'm dead. My father is dead. There's a price out on my head. But right now, I'm just missing my father." She drew in a slow breath, wishing she could settle her raw emotions. "When my mother died," she continued, "she had been sick for so long, and to be honest, her death came as a relief. It wasn't at all that I didn't miss her or that the pain wasn't real, but she was ready to go. But with my father… He ran a marathon three months before he died. I expected him to be around for a long, long time."

Ryan leaned forward in his hammock and caught her gaze. "I've always enjoyed the stories my father told about the two of them starting back from when they were in college." He let out a low laugh. "And don't forget all the practical jokes they pulled on our moms."

"Tried to pull," she said, smiling at the reminders. "I'm pretty sure they always got caught."

"I think you're right."

Her smile faded. "Do you know what's been the hardest?"

Ryan shook his head.

"I've never had the chance to talk to anyone about my father and what happened that day." She squeezed her eyes shut for a moment as the memories engulfed her. "I dream about what happened at night and relive the images during the day, and I know it sounds stupid, but it's like that day is locked up inside of me and I can't talk to anyone. I can't tell them what happened or work through the loss, because no one can know why I'm here. The only person who's known up until now is your father, and even he's a continent away. The last time I saw him, he was whisking me out of the country." She sucked in a breath of air. "Sometimes I just don't know how to get through this."

"There are no rules when it comes to grief. No right and wrong."

"I know."

"You can talk to me, Ellie. Tell me what happened."

She nodded, knowing she needed to find a way to let out the pent-up emotions. She started to tell him what had happened that day in short, emotionless sentences. The moment she'd realized something was wrong. When she found her father. The other man who'd been in the room. The smell of fire engulfing her. Escaping from the house and running for her life.

"I ran outside and managed to call your father. He saved my life, arranging for me to disappear. There had been missing evidence and threats against my father that had included myself. He was convinced they were going to come after me as well. Especially since I'd seen the man who killed my father."

"I'm so sorry for everything you've gone through."

"I think one of the hardest parts is that I've hardly had time to grieve. I wasn't able to go to his funeral. I never could visit his grave. I never really had the chance to say goodbye to him."

Ryan came over and kneeled down in front of her so he was at eye level. "Ellie, we're going to find a way to put an end to this. We're going to get you to Manaus, where we can catch a plane to São Paulo and then out of the country. I'm going to keep you safe."

Her eyes flooded with tears and the wall of emotion threatened to break and sweep over her like one of the waves from the river. "What if they find us? What if they find out Dr. Reynolds was helping me. I'm— I'm just so tired of running, but if anything happens to him…"

"You can't stay. Not when there is a price on your head and when everyone is out looking for you. We both know it won't be long until they find us again."

"I know, but what about the doctor? He's expecting us—"

"It's too risky after everything we've just gone through. They're not going to stop looking for us, which means we need to get out of here—somewhere safe—

and the sooner, the better. We'll figure out what to do about the doctor as soon as we're far enough away that they can't find us."

She looked into his blue eyes and felt her heart tremor. He'd swept in and rescued her, and in the process had turned out to be nothing like the annoying teenager she remembered. Instead, she'd trusted him with her life. But that didn't matter. There was no way she was going to let her heart get tangled up on top of everything else.

But the bottom line was a relationship between the two of them wasn't going to work out. Her head knew that. They had little in common, and she certainly had no desire to get involved with someone who spent his time at the bottom of the ocean and was gone for months at a time. He liked the adventure, and as far as she was concerned, she was perfectly happy with takeout and a movie on a Friday night, or spending a quiet afternoon at an art gallery.

She brushed away an unwanted tear. "I'm sorry. For the most part, I've been able to just keep looking ahead, but now…"

"It's normal. And you're exhausted for starters. You need to sleep."

"I know. Most of the time I'm strong. Mainly because I have to be. Then everything comes washing over me, and it's like I'm there again." She wiped her cheek with the back of her hand, wishing she could stop the tears. "And a part of me keeps asking if it's going to get better. When I'm going to stop crying at the drop of a hat and actually feel normal again."

Or maybe normal was something she should stop looking for.

* * *

He took her hands in his, wishing he could fix everything for her. Wishing he could ignore the growing feelings he had toward her. Because everything seemed wrong. Especially the timing. He didn't really know her anymore. Not really. What he did know, though, was while she saw herself as weak when she got emotional, he saw in her an amazing strength. She was willing to put the life of someone else above her own. And was willing to risk her own in the name of justice.

He ran his thumb across the back of her hand, surprised by the sudden surge of emotion by her nearness. And by the realization that he wanted to kiss her. Very badly. He reached up and brushed back her hair, aware that he was about to get his heart into trouble. Because while he might not have imagined falling for someone else, his fractured heart somehow felt whole when he was around her.

She looked up at him, eyes wide, but she didn't pull away. He brushed his lips across hers, then felt her react to the kiss. A moment later, he pulled back and breathed in the subtle scent of vanilla and Diego's homemade ant repellant. He let out a soft laugh.

"What's so funny?" she asked.

He smiled at her. "We both smell like ant repellant."

She matched his smile. "Yeah, I was just thinking the same thing."

His mind shifted back to the kiss. "Did I overstep my bounds?"

She shrugged but didn't look away. "I'm not sure yet. You came rushing in, saving the day like a knight on horseback, while everything I know is falling apart around me. To be honest, I'm struggling to know how to handle everything, including what I feel about you."

"I understand, but for me, you're not exactly that fourteen-year-old I liked to tease anymore. In fact, I'm feeling quite the opposite toward you."

She laughed.

"But if it's just me…" he continued, needing to hear he hadn't totally misread the signals.

"It's not just you. But with everything that's happened, I can't trust my emotions. I'm not even sure what I feel. We don't even know if we're going to get out of here alive. I feel like I'm on some roller-coaster ride and I can't get off. Maybe when this is over. I don't know."

"We're going to get out of here alive. I promise. And when we do, I think I just might ask you out on a proper date."

"Don't promise me things you can't control, Ryan." The hesitation was back in her eyes. "The authorities promised to keep my father safe after the threats he'd been receiving and now he's dead. These men don't play games. They play for keeps and somehow I—we—ended up in the middle of all of this."

The moment they'd just shared faded into the humid night.

"I'm scared of how this is going to end," she said.

"I know, but you're also exhausted. You need some sleep. We'll both feel better in the morning."

Her gaze shifted to the forest beyond them. "I'm not sure I can close my eyes. If they come looking for us tonight, I want to see them coming."

"Diego and his family promised to take turns keeping watch."

Ellie stifled a yawn, the fatigue from the day beginning to consume her. "I guess you're right, but you need to sleep as well."

"I know. And I will. And, Ellie…we'll find a way out of this. We have to. I really will do everything in my power to keep you safe."

He kissed her on the forehead, then moved back across the veranda to his hammock. A minute later she was lying down with her eyes closed. A sense of regret surfaced. He never should have mentioned how he felt. Not here. Not now. And she was right about another thing. He needed to sleep as well. But he had a feeling he'd dream about the beauty who'd somehow managed to capture his heart.

Ryan watched her until her breathing settled into an easy rhythm. The humidity was still heavy, but a breeze left over from the storm helped combat the heat. He could hear quiet voices talking from inside the house, and the river and sounds from the rain forest in the distance.

For the moment, they were safe, and that made him grateful for the family who'd agreed to take them in. But he also knew that word would travel fast and it wouldn't be long until those after them tracked them down. Which meant they couldn't stay here. They both needed to sleep, but before the sun rose in the morning, he wanted them as far away from here as possible.

A shadow appeared around the side of the house, then stopped a few feet from his hammock.

"Ryan?"

He squinted in the darkness. "Diego, is everything okay?"

The young man motioned him to the other side of the veranda, where they could talk without worrying about waking up Ellie.

"Is everything okay?" he asked again.

"Everything is fine, but…I need to talk to you about something."

Ryan stared out at the thick forested area surrounding the small compound, still worried they might find them. "Okay."

"I heard you talking about a doctor. Were you talking about Dr. Reynolds?"

Ryan hesitated with regard to the direction of the conversation and the wisdom of including Diego, but if they were going to get out of here, they were going to have to trust him.

"Ellie was planning to meet him. He had evidence on the man who killed her father, but we haven't been able to get ahold of him."

Diego nodded. "I know him. He is a good man who helps many of us. He spends one week every month at a clinic not far from here."

"We're worried that his life might be at risk," Ryan said.

"We could find him and take him with us."

Ryan shook his head. "We need to leave. Going and finding him would be dangerous and it would expose Ellie. We don't think they know who we were planning to meet."

"But if they do?" The young man stared at his shoes. "They kill people who get in the way. I've seen their bodies. Seen what they take. But most of all I'm tired of living in fear. Worried every day when I go out that the men who attacked me will return. Because next time,

"4 for 4" MINI-SURVEY

We are prepared to **REWARD** you with 2 FREE books and 2 FREE gifts for completing our MINI SURVEY!

FREE
Value Over
$20!

You'll get...

TWO FREE BOOKS & TWO FREE GIFTS

just for participating in our Mini Survey!

Dear Reader,

IT'S A FACT: if you answer 4 quick questions, we'll send you 4 FREE REWARDS!

I'm not kidding you. As a leading publisher of women's fiction, we value your opinions... and your time. That's why we are prepared to **reward** you handsomely for completing our mini-survey. In fact, we have 4 Free Rewards for you, including 2 free books and 2 free gifts.

As you may have guessed, that's why our mini-survey is called **"4 for 4".** Answer 4 questions and get 4 Free Rewards. It's that simple!

Thank you for participating in our survey,

Pam Powers

they might not leave me alive. Next time, they might hurt my family. I want to help stop them."

"I understand, because so do I, but we have no weapons, no authorities involved…nothing. And at this point, we're not even sure where the doctor is."

"I know we can't stop all of them, but they don't hesitate to kill over fuel or a cell phone."

"You have some kind of plan?" Ryan asked.

"The men who attacked me on the river, I've been following their boat for the past month. And I know where we can find them."

"You've been following them?"

"Once the authorities came, I knew I needed proof of what they were doing. Proof of where their hideouts are. Proof that would allow the authorities to put Arias and his men away for a very long time. If they took the doctor…"

Diego pulled out the cell phone he'd borrowed from a friend and started flipping through photos he'd taken. "I watched them overpower the men on this boat, all for a shipment of ice and salt. I have proof of drug transactions, and an attack on a tourist boat. They work for a man named Arias."

Ryan felt his jaw slacken. So he and Ellie had been right. Arias was behind the price on her head. "What do you know about him?"

"He's the leader of the cartels and has been working in this area for about six months. They're involved in all kinds of things. Drug running, extortion, raids… My family and the people of my village are all terrified to go out. I don't want to keep living like this. This is why I want to help. He gives the orders." Diego's eyes narrowed. "You know about him?"

Ryan nodded. "He's the one who ordered the hit on Ellie's father."

"If we're going to catch the guys who killed her father—if all of this is going to end—we need all the evidence we can get."

"But we're not going after these men ourselves." Ryan worked to weigh the pros and cons of going after the doctor. "I'll talk with Ellie in the morning, but if we do go after the doctor, that's all. We don't confront these men. We'll try to call him in the morning to find out where he is—first at the clinic—then after that we leave for the city together. Then leave the rest to the authorities."

And in the meantime, he was going to do a lot of praying that the decision to go after the doctor didn't backfire on them.

TEN

The sound of a howler monkey jerked Ellie from her sleep. She opened her eyes, confused for a moment as to where she was. The sun had almost made it to the horizon, leaving a hazy yellow film across the surrounding rain forest. Everything rushed back. The pirates, escaping into the river, Diego and his family's hospitality...

She glanced down at her wrinkled clothes that at least were dry now. She'd wanted to stay awake last night in case the men after them managed to track them down, but as much as she'd fought it, fatigue had overcome her. Besides, she knew that without sleep she wouldn't be worth anything. If they were going to ensure they got out of here, they needed to sleep.

She turned to the empty hammock on the other side of the veranda and felt her pulse race. Where was Ryan? She quickly swung her legs onto the wooden floor, then stopped as another memory flashed through her. She'd dreamed of him last night. Someone had been chasing them through the forests with a group of men close on their heels.

And then he'd kissed her.

She pressed the back of her hand against her lips.

But that part hadn't been a dream. They'd been talking, and Ryan had kissed her. And she'd kissed him back. In the middle of the Amazon rain forest. She glanced toward the house, still uncertain as to how she felt. Her emotions were wound tight, and she didn't know how to interpret them. Not now, anyway. Maybe he'd been right. Maybe one day when all of this was over, and she was able to stop running, she'd explore the feelings she might have toward him.

She shoved the thought out of her mind as she climbed out of the hammock. Her experience with Lance had taught her that things were rarely as they seemed. Men were quick to play with emotions, then leave you hanging. And yet somehow she'd totally missed all the signals. Besides, she and Ryan had nothing in common, and outside this twilight zone they'd fallen into, the two of them were complete opposites. She'd just have to chalk up the kiss to her letting her tangled emotions get the best of her.

Boards creaked beneath her feet as she walked across the veranda toward the front door of the house. Inside, Ryan stood in the middle of the room eating cut-up pineapple out of a bowl. And he was making her heart stir unexpectedly. She studied his strong jawline, well past any five-o'clock stubble, his bright blue eyes and the smile he wore when he saw her walk into the room. She reached automatically for her hair and tried to straighten the ponytail, wishing she could take a hot shower and at least change into some clean clothes. She had to look a sight after almost twenty-four hours in the jungle without a shower. Because swimming in the Amazon certainly didn't count.

"Good morning, sleepyhead."

"Hey…" She felt her cheeks blush and let her gaze sweep the floor. Maybe she was smitten. At least a little bit.

"Would you like something to eat?" He held out the bowl of pineapple. "This is incredible. Straight from a little field they have nearby."

"Thanks." She bit into a piece, then felt her mouth water. "Where is everyone?"

"Diego and his brothers went out to bring in some manioc."

"I didn't mean to sleep so long."

"They insisted you sleep—and I agreed—though we do need to go soon, as soon as you've eaten, but first… we need to talk about something."

A seed of fear sprouted in her gut. "Is everything okay?"

"For now." He grabbed another piece of pineapple. "Why don't we go outside. The sunrise is going to be beautiful this morning."

He led her back outside onto the veranda. The skies had completely cleared after last night's storms. The surrounding green of the forest glowed beneath the yellow haze of the sunrise.

Ryan leaned against the wooden railing. "Diego talked to me last night after you went to sleep."

She picked up another piece of pineapple. "About?"

"He's offered to take us to Manaus…but he's also offered to take us first to see if the doctor is at the clinic, since we haven't been able to get ahold of him."

"Is Diego involved in all of this? Is that wise? I don't want to be responsible for someone else getting hurt."

"I agree, but I'm pretty sure that without him, we won't find the doctor."

"You think we can trust him? There is a price for bringing us in."

"I do, actually. He has the same motivation you do. He has personal reasons for why he wants them stopped. And besides that, Diego told me he knows the doctor. He's done a lot for his village."

"I know. It's just that…"

She hesitated. She'd been the one who'd convinced Ryan to come with her. The one who'd gone against his father's advice and headed blindly into the rain forest looking for answers, only to discover there was a price on her head. The last thing they needed at this point was to trust the wrong person. The churning in her gut returned. Part of her wanted to simply call it quits and find the quickest way out of here. But she knew enough about Arias to know it wasn't going to just end. Not until one of them won.

He tilted up her chin with his thumb. "Hey, you've faced jumping off a boat into the Amazon and made it out of the jungle."

"That was running from danger. Now we're talking about running right into it."

"Diego's trying to get word to the authorities, but in the meantime, we're going to have to do this on our own."

"And if Dr. Reynolds isn't there?" She glanced across the veranda. Diego and his brothers had just arrived back. "If they've somehow found out he's involved in this?"

"We'll play it by ear, but we won't take any unnecessary risks."

"Okay."

"This is almost over."

"Is it?" She knew he was trying to reassure her, but after yesterday…

"We find the doctor, then head to Manaus with him. We're going to ensure Arias and his men pay for what they've done, Ellie. You'll be free again."

She nodded, ready to put this part of her life behind her. "I just thought of something else."

"What's that?"

"I need a piece of paper and something to draw with."

Ryan walked back into the house behind Ellie, curious as to what she was up to.

"Diego, do you have any paper and something I can write with?"

Diego hesitated in the middle of the living room. "Yes… I think I can find something."

"What are you thinking?" Ryan asked as Diego slipped out of the room.

"If I can make sketches of the men, Yuri, Pedro and the men on the boat, we'll have that much more evidence of who's behind this. Or maybe someone will recognize them. Especially if we have problems finding the doctor."

A minute later Diego came back out with a piece of paper and a worn pencil without an eraser. Ryan watched as Ellie grabbed the paper and pencil, laid the paper out on the table and started drawing.

"You are an artist?" Diego asked.

She nodded. "And I want to try to draw the men who took us. Yuri, Pedro and the leader of the pirates. We might need to show it to the authorities at some point. I also want to get it down on paper now, while their faces are still fresh in my mind."

Ryan watched her concentrate as she started sketching the outline of their faces, then began filling in the details. The likenesses, as the drawings came to life, were incredible.

Ten minutes later, she had her sketches. "This is Yuri and Pedro, the men who took us after our plane landed. And this is the leader of the pirates."

"Wow… I had no idea how good you were. And the details." Ryan held up the sketches, impressed with her talent. "It looks exactly like them."

"Before we go, I'd like to try to call the doctor."

Diego nodded and pulled his phone from his pocket, then handed it to her.

Ellie let the phone ring a dozen times before hanging up. "He isn't answering."

"There could be a number of explanations, Ellie. His phone could be dead, the cell towers could be down."

"He is right," Diego said. "Our cell-phone service is spotty out here."

"We can back out of this if that's what you want," Ryan said. "We can go straight to Manaus."

She shook her head. "Anything we do is a risk, but I need to make sure the doctor is okay."

Ryan nodded. "Then let's go."

An hour later, Ryan was sitting next to Ellie in the back of Diego's boat, surrounded by large bags of the starchy manioc root so no one could see the young man's passengers. He still questioned their decision to go after the doctor themselves, but Ellie had been right.

What other choice did they really have? It wasn't as if they could call 911 and send in the cavalry.

Diego tied their boat to a tree at the edge of the small town, hidden partially along the shoreline.

"I won't be long," Diego said from the shoreline. "No one should be able to see you, so you should be safe. And if the doctor is here, I'll try to get him to come back with me so you can talk with him."

"They might be watching the clinic," Ellie said.

"I'll be careful. I promise. Just stay out of sight."

Water lapped against the edges of Diego's dugout canoe, which had been equipped with a motor. Ryan glanced around the quiet place, wondering how the blue waters, covered partially with green plant life and surrounding forest, had suddenly become their place of refuge. Fishermen worked in the distance along the river. A boy paddled past in a small boat with an oar. No one seemed to notice their hiding place.

But even that didn't make him feel any better. He wished that they were already on their way to Manaus, or even yet on a plane taking them to somewhere—anywhere—safer than this.

The hour-long trip here had been uneventful, but that didn't keep him from continuing to glance over his shoulder and make sure they weren't being watched. But he knew that Diego had been right. Showing up in the middle of the village wouldn't be safe, either.

A dragonfly with a yellow head and a green-and-brown body landed on the edge of the boat, caught his attention, then flew away. There was no way that he and Ellie could simply blend with the locals. They were going to have to rely on Diego to get them the information they needed.

He swatted at another mosquito, ignoring the row of welts on his arms, then shifted his attention to Ellie, who sat across from him, drumming her fingers against her leg as she stared out across the river. Kissing her yesterday hadn't exactly been a part of the plan, but while he still wasn't sure what she thought about what had happened between them, he hoped she didn't regret it.

Maybe it had been a mistake. Getting involved with someone, even someone as beautiful and talented as Ellie, was something he needed to avoid.

"How are you feeling?" he asked, trying to find a way to break the silence that had settled between them.

"Let's just say I've decided that working at the bottom of the ocean might be less dangerous than trying to avoid a cartel leader."

He shifted, trying to find a more comfortable position on the wooden seat. "That and being eaten alive by every critter known to man."

She let out a low laugh. "I know I've done things in the past twenty-four hours I never imagined ever doing. Like jumping into the Amazon for starters."

Ryan matched her laugh. "You'll have quite a story for your grandchildren one day. We both will."

"This is one story I would have been happy to have skipped."

He noticed the blush that crept up her cheeks at the comment. Despite everything that had happened, there was one thing he didn't regret—reconnecting with Ellie. Still, he wished their kiss hadn't left such an awkwardness between them that apparently neither of them knew how to address. Which meant he needed to find a way to clear the air between them.

He drew in a deep breath. "I need to talk to you about something…about last night." He tried to keep his expression neutral. "When I kissed you, I crossed the line and I'm sorry. We've both got emotions running, and I never stopped to think through what I was doing."

Which wasn't exactly true. He'd known exactly what he'd been doing. She'd been completely irresistible with those wide eyes, a sunburn across her nose and that line of freckles across her cheeks. But he also knew it was far more than her looks that had somehow managed to needle their way into his heart. There was a strength about her that had impressed him. A desire to put the good of others above herself and protect them. Just like he wanted to do with her.

"Forget it. Seriously," she said. "You don't owe me an apology." She held up her hands and pointed to the forest around them. "I've realized that this isn't real life. At least it's not our life. This is more like we've fallen down some rabbit hole straight out of *Alice in Wonderland*. And while we're here, there's bound to be a few Mad Hatters showing up."

He couldn't help but smile. "Well, that's an interesting way to put it. Though I have to admit, I've thought once or twice about how I wished this was nothing but some crazy fantasy world we need to escape from."

"No kidding. My normal life is spent drawing in a studio and the most exciting thing I do is order something new off the menu at our local diner. But that's just it. You spend your days working at the bottom of the ocean and you enjoy it. You scuba dive for fun. We're too…different."

His smile faded. It would never work between them. That was what she was saying. And maybe she was right. But not for the reasons she was giving him. Or maybe she was just guarding her heart. She'd lost her father. Lost everything in her life that she'd known. Taking a chance with her heart had to feel like an impossible step.

Ryan shrugged. "I just didn't want things to be awkward between us."

"Seriously, there's no need to apologize. I appreciate all that you've done for me more than you will ever know, and hope we'll stay in touch once this is over."

He pushed aside any feelings he had toward her. It was time to drop the subject. "I still think your life has to be somewhat more rewarding than mine sometimes. My father told me you taught art-therapy classes."

"Was this when he was trying to convince you to come rescue me?"

"He spoke of you and your father often, actually, over the years. Tell me what's involved in the art therapy."

He noticed the muscles in her jaw seemed to relax and her shoulders loosened as if she was looking back at a good memory. He studied her face and waited for her to continue.

"Studies have found that in older adults, for example, art therapy can be very beneficial. It even helps them manage pain and memory loss."

"How is that?"

"When you challenge the mind doing things like painting and sculpting, it helps to promote cognitive abilities. And when dealing in memory loss, it seems to help the person focus. For example, when people are struggling to remember things, art can also calm them, and sometimes that's enough to bring them out of the fog."

"What you do sounds anything but boring, Ellie. Trust me. Though one day, I still want to take you diving with me."

"I'm pretty sure that won't happen." Her smile was back. "I've now had two diving encounters and both terrified me."

"Then I need to be the one to change that. It's beautiful down there. You'd love it. Trust me."

"It's not a matter of trusting you or not trusting you. It's just that…" She turned away before finishing her sentence. "Diego's back."

ELEVEN

Ellie felt her stomach clench as Diego approached them alone. Something wasn't right.

"Diego, did you find him?"

The young man shook his head as he stepped onto the boat. "The doctor is gone. I spoke to the young woman who works there. She told me he'd already left to go back to his village, and that he'd be back next month. She was closing the clinic until he returns."

Ellie shook her head as she glanced at Ryan, who, from his expression, looked just as concerned as she felt. "That doesn't make sense. Why would he leave early?"

Diego stopped next to her, then offered her a handful of Brazil nuts wrapped in paper. "I have no idea."

She took one of the nuts and popped it into her mouth. But at the moment, food was the last thing on her mind.

"Ellie…" Ryan studied her expression as he reached for one of the nuts. "What are you thinking?"

"That something's wrong. How did the woman seem?" she asked Diego.

"I don't understand."

"Did she seem scared or distracted?"

"I don't know. Maybe…scared."

"Do you think she was telling the truth? That he had just…left on his own?"

Diego hesitated again before answering. "I don't know."

"Here's what we do know," she said. "Dr. Reynolds wasn't supposed to leave yet. He only spent one week here every month, and unless there was an emergency he needed to tend to, I'm pretty sure he wouldn't leave early. If he's already gone, I don't think he left because he wanted to."

"You think they got him." Ryan's statement wasn't a question. It was the statement they'd all been thinking about. "Is your phone charged, Diego?"

"Yes." He pointed to his solar charger.

"We need to call the other clinic and confirm that he's there. If he left last night, he should already be back. If not…"

The boat bobbed in the tide while Diego made the call. Ellie gnawed at her lip. Things were getting complicated and their options were limited. Ryan had agreed to help her pick up the doctor on their way out of the country, but now they didn't even know where he was. Or where the evidence they needed was. She grabbed another nut and chomped down on it. Ryan's father wasn't going to be happy when he found out what they were doing, but she hoped that he would also understand her insistence at not leaving the doctor behind. Especially if he was in trouble. She needed this to be over. Which meant they had to find him and his evidence. And ensure nothing happened to him.

A boat sailed past them on the water. Her heart raced

as she pressed into the shadows and studied the passengers. But they were only fishermen, seemingly uninterested in a boat full of manioc bobbing along the shoreline. When was she going to be able to stop looking over her shoulder?

Diego ended his call a second later. "You were right. The doctor is not there. He never showed up."

"He wouldn't have just left." She caught Ryan's gaze. "Not unless he was forced to leave. Not unless they took him."

His frown deepened, and she could tell he wasn't ready to go there. "It's possible, but you're drawing conclusions, Ellie, that may or may not be true. You told me you were careful to ensure no one knew you were coming to meet with him. How would they find him?"

"I don't know, but think about it. How long would it take to figure out why I was coming here?"

"She has a point," Diego said. "Dr. Reynolds is the only foreigner who comes here regularly for miles. It makes sense that they would at least question him."

She pressed her lips together, weighing their options. "If they took the doctor, someone had to have seen something."

"What are you suggesting?" Ryan asked. "That we start canvasing the town? In case you forgot, there's a price out on our heads. We shouldn't even be out here."

"I didn't forget, but what do you suggest? I need to find him. I'm the one who convinced him he was doing the right thing. I can't walk away now. I owe it to the doctor."

Ryan clearly wasn't convinced. "Going back to the clinic's too risky, Ellie."

But she wasn't going to back down. How could she? She wasn't going to just walk away from this, and she certainly wasn't going to walk away if she thought someone was in danger. Even if it meant risking her own life in the process.

"My cousin lives on the water a few minutes down-river," Diego said. "The town is small. If something happened, she will know."

She turned to Ryan. "Okay?"

He paused for a moment, then nodded his head. "Okay."

A minute later, Diego eased the boat back out into the water, quickly leaving behind the small town that wasn't much more than a dot on the map. A series of small islands strung out on their left. River otters swam in the water, while a man rowed a boat past them carrying bags of manioc flour.

She glanced at Ryan. She knew he wasn't happy with her insistence to go after the doctor. And maybe he was right. The longer they stayed here, the greater the chance became of them being found. But she needed to see if the doctor was okay.

Diego headed toward the shore, to a painted blue house with stilts that kept the structure out of the swollen river when the water rose. Laundry had been strung out on a long cord, while a skinny dog slept on the porch. It was a scene completely contrary to a city like Rio, where she'd spent the past few months.

"I think it's safe for you to come out. We're far enough out of town." Diego jumped out of the boat ahead of them, calling out to his cousin in Portuguese. "Paula… are you here?"

A little girl ran out of the house, then quickly stepped back into the shadows when she saw them approaching.

A younger woman then hurried out and came down the stairs with a baby on her hip. "Diego, what are you doing here?"

"I want you to meet two of my friends." Diego quickly made introductions, then continued in Portuguese. "We came to find the doctor, but he's not at the clinic. Do you know where he is?"

The woman looked barely twenty and already had a baby and a toddler. "I heard there was an emergency at his other clinic down the river and he had to leave."

The woman knew something. Ellie could see it in her eyes.

"Are you sure?" She glanced back toward the river, praying that what she was doing didn't get the woman into any kind of trouble. "I was supposed to meet the doctor. We had something…important to discuss. I need to find him. But if something has happened…if he's in some kind of trouble—"

"Like I told you, the doctor left to go home. That's all I know."

"What is she saying?" Ryan asked.

"That she doesn't know anything," Ellie said. "But I don't believe her. Something's wrong." She turned back to Paula. "I don't think that's what happened. I think someone took him or forced him to leave with them. Is that what happened? It's a small town. News travels fast—"

"No." Paula pulled the baby tighter against her chest.

"Paula, there are some very bad men out there that

we are trying to stop. If the doctor is in trouble, we want to help him. But we can't if we don't know where he is."

"I…" Paula looked back toward the house, her voice barely above a whisper. "If I tell you…if they find out I saw them…"

"Please tell us what happened," Ellie said. "It's important."

"It's not the first time they have come."

Ellie glanced at Ryan and started translating as Paula spoke. "These people mainly strike at night. Like Diego told us before, they attack boats and take what they want, but they also come here. And because the police boats rarely make it here, we have no one to protect us. And they know it."

"And these men," Ellie said. "They took the doctor?"

"They came to the clinic yesterday and grabbed him."

"Who grabbed him?"

"Three men with guns. They didn't even worry about hiding or coming at night."

"Do you know where they went?"

"They got into a boat and headed down the river. People saw what they did, but even that didn't stop them. There is nothing we can do. They have guns. We have nothing. We just give them what they want and pray that they leave."

"Maybe there is something you can do," Ellie said.

The woman's eyes still held the terror of what had happened. "What do you mean?"

"You're a witness. The other men and women in the town are all witnesses."

"Yes, but like I said, the authorities rarely come here. And if we turn them in, they will make us pay."

"Would you recognize the men if you saw them again?"

She pressed her lips together and nodded.

Ellie pulled the sketches out of her back pocket, unfolded the paper and held it up. "I know this is hard, but did you see any of these men?"

Paula pressed her hand against her mouth and nodded before pointing to the sketch. "This man."

Ellie nodded. "He led the pirate boat that took us."

"Do you think they'll hurt him?" Paula asked. "Because Dr. Reynolds comes every month to treat the people of this town. My baby would have died without his medicine."

Ellie sent up another prayer for the doctor. "I don't know what they're going to do, but that's why we're here. We're going to do everything we can to put a stop to this."

She glanced toward the river. "There's something else you need to know."

"What is it, Paula?"

"These men have no fear. And they are looking for both of you. If one of us turns you in, there will be a reward. It isn't safe for you to stay."

She quickly translated for Ryan as Paula hurried back up the stairs and into her house. "I don't know what to do, but we need to find him, Ryan."

"Agreed."

Diego swatted at a mosquito that had landed on his arm. "I think I might know where he is."

"Wait a minute." Ryan stepped up next to Diego as Paula disappeared into her house with her baby and toddler. "How?"

"I didn't tell you everything last night," Diego said. "After I was attacked, I knew I couldn't wait for the authorities to get here. I started hunting *them* down. I especially wanted to find out where their camps were located along the river."

"And you found that evidence?" Ryan asked.

"Four days ago, I discovered one of their camps a few miles down the river."

"If they have the doctor," Ellie said, "it would make sense that they would take him there."

"What kind of setup do they have?" Ryan asked Diego.

"I've been there the past few nights. I've seen five men and at night they typically leave the camp empty except for a couple of women, who cook and wash for them. Sometimes they come back after a few hours. Sometimes they stay out until the next morning. From what I've learned, they've been there about three weeks now. I've been told they move their camp from time to time so they can hit a new section of the shoreline, but they know this river better than most people. Which is why it's so easy for them to vanish."

Ryan studied Ellie's reaction. He knew what she was thinking. Already too many people had been hurt in this play for power that seemed to have spread all the way to the Amazon. Getting Diego involved meant one more person, but as far as he was concerned, Diego and his family were already involved. And if they could find Dr. Reynolds...

"We need to call the authorities," Ellie said. "Diego, if you can show them where these men are, surely they will come—"

"I have, and they will come. Eventually," Diego said. "But they have hundreds of square miles of this forest to protect and are spread out far too thin. It could be days before anyone shows up."

Ellie caught Ryan's sleeve. "By then—if he's there—it will be too late to save him."

"I agree," Ryan said, "but neither can we just walk into their compound and expect them to let us take him with us. If we're going to do this, we need some kind of plan."

"How far to their camp?" Ellie asked.

"Not too far," Diego said.

Paula called out to Diego from the top of the wooden staircase.

"I'll be back in a few minutes," Diego said.

"What do you think?" Ellie asked, once the Brazilian was out of earshot.

Ryan tried to read her expression. "I think we're outmanned and outgunned. We need to get out of here and let the authorities deal with this. Because while I understand that the doctor's life is on the line, they're out there looking for us. Eventually, word is going to leak out that we're here."

"I know, but if we do nothing…"

She let her voice trail off. He could read the conflict in her eyes. She wanted to go after the doctor, but at the same time they all knew the dangers in taking on these men. But he also knew that there was more involved than saving the doctor's life. Her life hung in the balance as well.

"You make the call, Ellie. Though I suppose I don't have to ask you to know your answer. We can leave for Manaus now and try to keep out of sight, or take a chance of getting caught and attempt to rescue the doc."

"I don't know. Part of me thinks we never should have come here."

"Quit second-guessing yourself. All along you've done what you believed to be right. Not just justice for yourself, but for your father, for the doctor and now for the people here."

She shot him a smile. "Why does it seem like all of a sudden that you're the one rallying us forward to save the doc?"

He let out a chuckle. "I guess you did a good job convincing me."

"You think we can pull this off?"

"I think we have to be smart. We can go in first and scout out the situation. It's hard to judge until we get there, but if Diego's right, and we wait until nightfall, we might be able to get in and get out without much resistance."

He watched her struggle with her decision as he wrestled with his own concerns. Part of him felt compelled to at least try to rescue the doctor. It was the right thing to do. Not only could they potentially save a man's life, but with the evidence Diego had, they could also put away Arias for good.

But he didn't want to involve Ellie. The problem was, neither did he feel comfortable in leaving her somewhere. Not that he thought she couldn't handle herself. She was resourceful. There was no doubt about that. But staying together seemed wiser. If he judged they could get in and get out with little or no resistance, it was going to be worth going in. He just didn't want to do anything to jeopardize her safety. That was something he wasn't willing to do.

Which showed him just how much his heart was getting involved.

He shoved away the thought. He'd lost someone he cared for before and he had no desire to go there again. But he also didn't want her to feel forced into a corner.

"Ellie, leaving here doesn't mean quitting. And it doesn't mean failure. If we can get to the city, we can still work to get the authorities back here. They'll be much more prepared to handle a situation like this."

"But we're running out of time and risk losing the doctor that way."

He glanced behind her, toward the river, which at the moment was quiet without any boats. Either way was a gamble. He knew that. Taking risks was part of his job. He'd learned to weigh the pros and the cons before going in. They had to do the same today.

"You've talked to me about your job," she said. "About the risks and the rewards. Do you ever let your doubts stop you?"

"When I'm down on the bottom of the ocean? No. I remind myself that what I'm about to do is crazy. I know what has to be done, but I also know our limits and never push them."

"And our limits today?" she asked.

"We have to make sure Diego's right about the guards. See if we can identify how many are there, if there are any guards left behind. If we go at night, there's a better chance no one sees us or the fact that we're not from around here. We make sure the odds are in our favor before we strike. Otherwise we don't go in."

"My father used to tell me that if I decided to do something, I needed to jump in all the way. No looking back. I just— I just don't want to lose someone else."

He liked the way she looked at a problem. She wasn't willing to jump in without intelligently weighing the risks, but neither was she going to let fear stop her.

Like losing Heather had stopped him from living.

He tried to push down the memories, but this time couldn't. What happened with Heather was something he rarely, if ever, talked about, even with his father and his best friend back home.

"Ryan?"

He hesitated. "Earlier, you asked me if I'd ever lost anyone unexpectedly."

She nodded, then waited for him to continue.

"I lost someone once." He stared out at the river. "Her name was Heather. Long story short, we started dating and after six months I asked her to marry me." Ryan hesitated again before continuing. "We planned a Christmas wedding up in the mountains, and you can only imagine how my mother wanted to be involved in every detail. I was actually surprised she didn't end up running Heather off."

He frowned as more memories rose to the surface. "Two weeks before the wedding, she was on her way to an appointment with the caterer and a drunk driver slammed into her car. She was killed instantly at the scene."

Ellie pressed her hand against her lips and shook her head. "Oh, Ryan, I'm so sorry. I remember my father telling me something had happened and the wedding was off, but I didn't remember that."

"For the first few weeks, I was inundated with calls, emails and even personal visits from friends and co-workers. Everyone was horrified at what had happened. At the funeral, people told me all kinds of things at the time. She was in a better place. I'd eventually get over her and find someone else."

All clichés he'd dismissed at the time. He'd felt numb, disoriented at the fact that what he'd planned for his life had completely changed.

"Tell me about her," Ellie said.

"We met in Denver shortly after I left the navy. She was training for a marathon."

"She must have been quite an athlete."

"She was. Her goal was to run the Kauai Marathon in Hawaii, which is one of the hardest in the US."

Her focus and determination were what he'd first noticed in Heather. Qualities that Ellie held as well. He shook off the comparison.

"When I got the call that she'd been in an accident... it was like my world just fell off its axis. I couldn't imagine that she was gone. You mentioned feeling invincible. I guess I thought we were. In my mind, I saw us having a family and growing old and taking on the world together. No matter what you see on the news every day. People die, life is fragile. You just never think that it could happen to you. That everything could be lost in one fatal moment. A month later I signed on as a saturation diver."

"And today...after some time has passed, do you feel as if you're starting to heal?"

When he hesitated, she kept speaking. "I guess I'm

asking because right now I'm not sure I see my own heart healed."

"As much as I didn't want to hear it back then—I came to realize that while she'll always have a place in my heart, I had to move on. I look at my future differently and have accepted that it won't be with her. But as for moving on… Yeah. I'd say I have."

He shoved his hands into his pockets, wondering how he was at the point where he was talking about Heather in the middle of the Amazon. "That was two years ago. And—according to my father—I'm still running. Maybe he's right. I don't know. I just knew I didn't know how to keep doing what I was doing with reminders of her everywhere I went. But moving on? Yes. Has the pain eased? Yes. Falling in love again…"

He hesitated, wondering why he'd brought that up. After Heather, he'd never found anyone he'd even considered wanting to spend a lifetime with. Until now. He shook off the thought. He needed to focus on what he had to do right now to ensure he kept her safe. "We need to make sure no one else gets hurt," he said.

"You're sure about this?"

He nodded. "We need to wait until dark, then go after the doctor."

TWELVE

Ellie watched the river ripple behind them in the wake of the boat, while Ryan sat across from her, his jaw taut. She wasn't sure if his serious expression came from their decision to continue the mission of trying to find the doctor, or because it had dredged up memories of loss. *That* she could understand—the physical ache that often went with losing someone you love. And so far, for her, it had yet to fade. But hearing his story about Heather had also done something else. It had opened up another layer of who Ryan was. And somehow sprouted a new desire inside of her to get to know the man.

But she couldn't think about that right now. Even after spending the day waiting at Paula's for night to fall, she still found that her nerves were shot and her heart wouldn't stop pounding. She needed to stop second-guessing their decision, but slipping into the rabbit hole had now become more like an episode of *The Twilight Zone*. Her routine life had managed to morph into something totally out of control, and she had no idea when it was going to stop. She stared out across the mesmerizing waters as they sped past miles of green forest. Losing her mother had been her first real experience with tragedy and loss. And with that loss had come a redefining of who she was and what was important. And then the unimaginable had happened, and she'd lost her father. It had changed her perspective and shifted her priorities. Which was why she couldn't just walk away.

She shot up another prayer, keeping up with her continual dialogue with God. They needed to find the doctor quickly and get out. Diego's assurances, though, that the camp wasn't well guarded did little to convince her that they hadn't made a risky decision. If Arias ended up showing up, or if they were confronted by armed men... She reined in her train of thought. She wasn't even going to go there. She couldn't. Because not going wasn't an option.

"The sky's incredible, isn't it?"

At Ryan's question, she shifted her attention to the sunset. "Yes, it is."

She might have been looking out across the water, but she hadn't really seen anything. At the moment, the river looked like a sea of glass, with the yellow glow of the sinking sun reflecting against it. Wispy clouds hovered above the horizon. If she closed her eyes, she could almost imagine it was just the two of them, lost in this world. A world where no one was after them. Or maybe that was just what she wanted.

She pushed away the unrealistic thoughts.

"One day I want to come back here and really see the rain forest. Without worrying that beyond every turn in the river, there's someone after us."

A chill rushed up her spine. There was no way to forget what was real at this moment.

"You okay?" he asked.

"Depends on the minute, I guess."

"That's understandable." He leaned forward, brushing his fingers across her knees. "I'm a hundred percent behind us rescuing the doctor, but if you want to back out—"

"No. I still want to do this. I know it's the right thing to do."

No matter what happens. But the distraction of the setting sun wasn't enough to settle the turmoil raging inside her.

She turned to Diego, who was guiding his boat. She needed an answer to the question that had been hovering at the back of her mind all day. "Diego?"

He glanced back at her, his hand still firm on the tiller.

"If Arias was to show up, how would he get in and out of here?" She hadn't been able to shake the feeling that he might come after them in person.

"You think he would risk coming here?" Diego asked.

"I don't know, but if he did. How would he get here?"

They'd discussed Arias over lunch today. The men working for him seemed inept at what they did, their only motivation a pocketful of money. But from the details she knew about the case, Arias was different. He had no problem paying men to do his dirty work, but neither would he hesitate to get a job done himself. She glanced behind her for signs of another boat, wishing she could shake the unease that had settled in her stomach. She couldn't exactly imagine the man coming here after her. After her father's death, the cartel leader had been released from prison on a technicality. Which meant his best bet was to simply disappear.

But she'd seen photos of his four-million-dollar mansion. It was nestled in a gated community outside Dallas and included an indoor heated pool, a sauna and four fireplaces. She also knew he wasn't going to take a chance that evidence might show up that would send him back to prison.

Diego seemed to ponder her question. "My guess would be that he'd fly in, then take a boat the rest of the way like you did."

"What about the road system?" Ryan asked above the low roar of the motor. "Is that a viable option?"

"Yes, but the construction is a never-ending job," Diego said, "Which is why most people use the river. Many of the sections aren't even completed yet and are nothing more than dusty roads in the dry season and a muddy mess in rainy season. They build the roads primarily for oil, gas and logging companies, but the cowboys use them as well to drive their herds of cattle. They're just not practical for most people.

"Do you think he will show up?" Diego asked.

Ryan shook his head. "Impossible to say, really. But if he's the one who put out a bounty on us, and he realizes he still doesn't have us…"

Diego steered the boat toward the shoreline. "The camp's a little bit farther up the river, but we can walk from here."

Ryan took Ellie's hand and helped her out of the boat and onto the waterlogged shoreline. He squeezed her hand before letting go, leaving goose bumps up and down her arm. She shoved away the distraction as they started walking parallel to the shoreline toward the camp, careful to keep in the shadows of the forest.

They'd agreed not to use flashlights, which meant the only light came from the now setting sun and the faint glow of the moon.

The sound of a motor hummed in the distance, growing louder. Ryan held up his hand, and she froze behind him and Diego. A mosquito buzzed in her ear, but she hardly noticed it. Instead, she drew in a sharp breath as the familiar silhouette of the pirate's boat sped past them. Ryan grabbed her hand.

"That's them," Diego said. "They're leaving now."

The three of them stood in silence until the boat vanished into the darkening waters.

"How long do you think we have until they return?" Ryan asked.

"Several hours. Maybe until morning."

Plenty of time for them to get in and out. That knowledge gave her a sense of relief. But only if the men stuck to their routine.

She walked between Ryan and Diego as they headed toward the camp, thankful for the cover of darkness. Five minutes later, they were close enough to scout out the compound, but deep enough in the shadows that they wouldn't be spotted. Her heart raced as she took in the four wooden structures, far enough off the river that you wouldn't see them from a boat passing by. She watched for movement among the shadows.

"I see a woman," Ryan said.

"She will be the one who does the cooking and washing for the men," Diego said.

"There's a guard at two o'clock," Ryan said, "but he's armed."

"If we take him by surprise, we can take him down."

Diego crouched down beside them. "We've got a couple of machetes and a length of rope."

Great. So they'd brought a knife to a gunfight. Even at three against one, she didn't like the odds. But it wasn't as if there were a pile of options.

Ellie started searching the row of small huts for the doctor and signs of another guard. Something moved on the side of the second building. Dr. Reynolds sat on a chair against the wall, his hands tied behind him.

"The doctor's here," Ellie said, blowing out a sigh of relief. "But what about the woman? Do you think she'll be a problem?"

"I don't think so," Diego said. "She's probably either a relative or someone they are keeping against her will."

They watched the guard's movements for another fifteen minutes, but clearly security wasn't something he was worried about.

"Ellie." Ryan squeezed her hand. "I want you to go to the woman. Keep her quiet and make her understand that we're not here to hurt her. We'll take care of the guard. Are you good with that?"

She nodded. "Yes."

"Diego, let's go."

Ellie kept to the shadows as she crossed the compound in the opposite direction of Ryan and Diego to where the woman was washing dishes.

The woman saw her and Ellie started toward her.

"Senhora…" She needed to keep the woman quiet.

The woman screamed and started running.

"Senhora, no—"

Someone flew at her from behind, slamming into her, and knocked her to the ground.

* * *

Ryan grabbed the unsuspecting guard from behind and quickly wrapped his arm around the man's neck. His weapon dropped to the ground. A second later, Ryan had him subdued. He signaled for Diego to tie up the man, then froze. Shouts sounded across the compound. He glanced back to where Ellie had gone, then felt his stomach drop. There was a second guard standing over someone.

Ellie.

Grabbing the gun, he sprinted across the compound. Where had the second guard been? Ellie was facedown on the ground, but he couldn't tell if she had been hurt. He aimed his gun at the man's head.

"Put your gun down," Ryan shouted.

Diego came up behind him, yelling in Portuguese at the man, who had yet to move.

The guard lunged at Ryan. Using the momentum of his punch, he pulled the man toward him, then swept his leg around, knocking him to the ground. He tried to scramble to his feet, but Ryan knocked him out with a punch square to the jaw.

He grabbed the second gun, then shouted at Diego to tie the man up.

"Ellie…" He helped her back up onto her feet and pulled her into his arms. They'd cut this one way too close. "You okay?"

Ellie rubbed her wrist and nodded as Diego started tying up the second guard with the rope they'd brought. "Yeah. I think so."

"Good, because we need to hurry. I don't want to take any chances of the others coming back before we get out of here. Make sure both of the guards can't escape, Diego, and Ellie and I will go get the doctor."

"Dr. Reynolds…" Ellie said a moment later. "I'm Ellie Webb."

The doctor looked up at them. "Ellie?"

"Are there any other guards?" Ryan asked.

"No, just the two of them."

"Well, then, the cavalry has arrived," she said, shooting the doctor a smile. "Or at least we've arrived."

"Ellie, I can't believe it. You found me."

She quickly made introductions, then studied the older man's face in the moonlight. He had a large bruise across his left cheek and a long red gash across the edge of his receding hairline.

"They did this to you?"

"It's nothing."

Her stomach lurched. "I'm so sorry."

Ryan started cutting through the ropes that secured his hands behind him with one of the machetes.

Ellie stopped in front of him. "I'm so, so sorry. This is all my fault."

"No, it's not. I agreed to help you. I wanted to help you. I just thought… I didn't think they'd find me. I tried to be so careful. At least you're alive. They told me they were going to kill you."

"That was their plan, I'm sure, but we managed to escape."

"Can you tell us what happened?" Ryan asked as she started on the man's bound feet.

The doctor glanced around him, clearly nervous. "I always knew that if they found out what I'd done, they would kill me, but I decided I had to take the risk. Two years ago, Arias's men killed my son. To this day, it's an unsolved case, but I know who did it. Not a day goes by that I don't wish I had a way to avenge his death. That is why I take the risk. That is why I decided I will do anything I can to stop these men."

"I understand your loss," Ellie said, "and I am so sorry."

"I never met your father, but I read about him in the newspaper. I realized he was willing to stand up against evil. Somehow it gave me the courage to try to help put an end to what is going on here when I heard from you. Yesterday, they came to my clinic. They didn't even try to hide. They just walked in like they owned the place, put a gun to my head and told me I was coming with them. They dragged me away to one of their boats, knowing no one would stop them."

"And since you've been here?" Ryan finished with the second rope and pulled it off.

"They've been questioning me." He shoved his wire-framed glasses up the bridge of his nose, then rubbed his wrists. "But I insisted I didn't know where you were. And I didn't tell them anything."

"You did fine," Ellie said.

The doctor glanced toward the river and started to stand but quickly fell back down onto the chair.

"Dr. Reynolds?" Ellie grabbed the older man's arm.

"I'm okay." He held up his hand. "I haven't moved for hours, and I'm stiff and probably dehydrated. I just need a minute, but we need to leave. If they come back and find me missing, they will come after me. And we all know they won't stop there."

"I saw some water around the corner," Ellie said. "I'll be right back."

Ryan squatted down in front of him. "Our friend over there has a boat and can get us to Manaus. And once we're there, we can get a plane out of the country."

"I have the evidence Ellie needs." The doctor pulled out a small ziplock with a folded paper inside it from the bottom of his shoe as Ellie returned with a cup of water.

"Where did you find it?" Ryan asked.

"About a month ago, I treated a man for a ruptured appendix that almost cost him his life. Inside the man's clothing, I found a small book filled with handwritten lists of narcotics dealers, surveillance reports, hits and the names of dirty law enforcement officers here, in the United States and in Venezuela. I copied it, then carefully tucked it back away, praying no one would be the wiser."

The doctor handed Ellie the paper, then took a sip of the water she offered. "Your father's name is there on the list of hits. It's proof that Arias was behind this."

"This is enough information to put Arias and his men away for the rest of their lives," Ryan said.

Ellie took a step backward into better light and stumbled.

"Are you okay?" Ryan asked.

She nodded, brushing off his question, but he didn't miss the pain in her eyes. "I twisted my ankle when I fell, but it's nothing."

"Let the doc take a look at it."

"Really, Ryan. I'm fine. It's nothing more than a sprain."

"No, he's right. Let me quickly take a look at it, then I think I'll be able to go."

Ellie hesitated, then let him look.

"Did you hear a pop or a snap when you hit the ground?" he asked.

"No. Which is why I really don't think it's broken. I can move it. It just hurts when I walk."

Ellie sat on a wood chair and the doctor kneeled down in front of her and pulled off her tennis shoe.

The doctor pressed along the side of her ankle. "Where does hit hurt?"

Ellie winced. "Ouch."

"That answers my question. But it doesn't seem crooked, and it doesn't seem to be swelling much. Just a bit discolored on the side. Can you move it?"

Ellie nodded and moved it in a slow circle.

"What about pressure on it if you stand?"

"Let me try."

Ryan reached out and grabbed her arm, helping her balance. "Well?"

Ellie's jaw tensed. "I really think it's okay. The pain's not that bad."

"You don't look okay," the doctor said, "but I don't think it's broken, just sprained, though walking could make it worse. And the only way to really tell is with an X-ray, which, of course, we don't have access to. What you really need is an ice pack, and I don't have one of those, either."

"I'll be fine," she said, putting her shoe back on. "We need to get out of here. Once we get to Manaus, I can find some ice."

"I've double-checked the guards," Diego said, walking up to them. "Neither of them are going anywhere."

"And the woman?"

"I let her go," Diego said. "She was being held against her will and was grateful."

"Then all we have to do is get to the boat," Ryan said.

"Ryan…"

He turned toward the river at Ellie's warning and heard the buzz of a motor. A second later he caught the reflection of lights on the water. Someone was out there.

"We need to hurry."

Ryan wrapped his arm around Ellie's waist. They headed for the shadows of the forest. He was sure she was walking as fast as she could, but it wasn't fast enough.

"I'm going to carry you."

"Ryan—"

The sound of a rifle fired in the air behind them. Ryan tightened his hold on Ellie.

"Turn around slowly," someone shouted, "and put your hands up in front of you."

Frustration coursed through him. Five men with weapons stood in a semicircle around them. They'd been so close. All they needed to do was get to the boat, then head up the river.

He turned around, his arm still wrapped around Ellie's waist. He felt her fingers dig into his skin. He couldn't let anything happen to her. His job was to protect her. He'd promised his father. Promised himself he wouldn't let this happen again.

Ellie drew in a sharp breath as one of the men stepped into the moonlight in front of them. "Arias."

THIRTEEN

Ellie took a step backward, wincing as the pain shot up her leg. But she couldn't worry about that. Not at the moment. She glanced at Diego, her suspicions rising. Had this been a trap all along? Had he been bought out like the others and brought them here, knowing Arias was coming? She tried to dismiss the suspicions, but she couldn't. Not completely.

Arias's men untied the two guards, clearly irritated.

"They sneaked up on us and had weapons—"

"Shut up," Arias shouted in Portuguese. "I'll deal with both of you later."

Ryan took a step forward. "Let her go—"

Arias held up his rifle and grinned. "Unfortunately, you're not the one giving the orders right now. I am. Which means the three of you are going to do exactly what I say."

"Ryan…"

She caught the fear in his eyes and looked away.

Arias signaled to one of his men to search them. One of them found the folded piece of paper from the doctor's pocket and pulled it out.

"You idiots never even thought to check his pockets when you grabbed him?"

Arias proceeded to slide it out of the ziplock bag, then frowned. "So Lucus thought he had to take out insurance and keep a record of my sins."

She caught the look in Ryan's eye. Arias had just found their evidence. The one thing they had tying him to her father's murder. And without that evidence they had nothing.

"I'm sorry, but I'm going to have to dispose of your 'evidence.'" Arias laughed as he pulled a box of matches out of his pocket, lit one of them against the box, then burned the paper. Seconds later, the orange flame devoured the list and black ashes dropped to the ground. "We wouldn't want it to get into the hands of the wrong people, now would we?"

Ryan took a step forward. "This isn't over—"

"Forget it. You've lost, and I've won. It's over. Or it will be soon. We found the boat you came in. I want the three of you to get back into that boat now." Arias nodded at Ryan, Diego and the doctor, then addressed one of his men. "You know what to do."

The man nodded. "Everything is ready."

"And you…" He pointed to Ellie. "You're coming with me."

"Ryan…"

Arias grabbed her arm and aimed his weapon at her as he let out a low laugh. "Forget it. Your boyfriend won't be coming to the rescue this time, because if you try to do anything, I will shoot her. She knows I don't have any problem with that, don't you?"

Ellie watched as Arias's men led Ryan and the others toward the boat. She had no idea what he was planning, but whatever it was, they needed to stop things now. But Arias wasn't someone simply working for a boss. He *was* the boss.

She watched in a panic as they shoved the men onto the boat. She knew their plan had been risky, but this wasn't supposed to have happened.

"What are you doing with them?"

"You fool. You never should have come here. Never should have tried to take things into your own hands."

"Let me go." She tried to pull away, but he only gripped her arm tighter.

"Forget it, you're coming with me and this time there will be no chance to escape. Because this time, I'm going to take care of this myself. And you're going to make sure I make it out of here."

His words sliced through her like an icy wind. Because she knew he was right. Knew Arias wasn't going to let her leave here alive. He'd use her as long as he needed her, then kill her.

"What are you going to do?" she asked.

"Make sure this all ends once and for all." He kicked at the small pile of ashes on the ground. "Starting with the doctor and your boyfriend. You all thought you were so clever with this list of names. You think it will actually work? I know enough people who can make sure this is over. You can't win."

"You don't know that." She watched as they shoved Diego's boat out onto the water. What were they doing?

"That's why I'm going to guarantee none of you ever have the chance to get in the way."

Ellie glanced around her. The river was in front of

them, but twenty yards to her left was the entrance of the forest. She had to run. Take a chance that Arias wasn't a good shot when it came to a moving target. But with her ankle she wasn't sure it was possible. An explosion rocked the boat before she could make her next move.

Ellie let out a scream. "What have you done?"

His fingers pressed into her arm, shooting pain up her elbow, but she barely felt it. "I only need one of you."

Ellie jerked away from his grip, ignoring the pain as she ran toward the boat, but Arias was faster. Smoke curled up from the water above the orange flames licking at the boat where Ryan, Diego and the doctor had just been as Arias grabbed onto her again.

Anger coursed through her. She spun around and jabbed her elbow into his throat. He groaned, then stumbled backward, almost losing his balance. She started running again, but he grabbed her arm, wrenching it behind her back as the boat burned.

Ryan couldn't be dead. It wasn't possible. And the doctor and Diego…

She turned around at another explosion that ripped through what was left of the boat.

Ellie stared at the wreckage. "You killed them."

"And if I hadn't, then where would I be right now? There's no way I'm going back to prison. Not here, not in the US…"

She stumbled backward and fell, skinning her elbow on a rock in the process. Drops of blood dripped down her arm from the scrape, but she didn't feel anything. Instead, a numbness swept through her as she watched the flames soar above the boat that was disintegrating into the water.

"You just don't give up, do you?" he said, pulling her up.

Ellie tried to pull away, but it was useless. "What do you want?"

"Besides my freedom?" Arias shot her a wicked smile. "You and your father have done enough to mess up my life. It's time to put all this behind me."

"You didn't have to kill my father. All he was doing was his job."

"It worked, didn't it? I got off free and clear."

"Because of some technicality, not because you deserve to be free."

And now Ryan, Diego and the doctor were dead.

"Like father, like daughter, I guess. You put your nose into someone else's business and bad things happen. But don't worry. All of this will be over soon. You and your boyfriend should never have interfered. There's just one more thing I need from you."

"How did you find out I was alive?"

"I have sources everywhere, though sadly—for you—you won't be around to find out."

His fingers tightened against her arm as they headed back toward the compound. Her father had been right. There had been a leak. Someone working for Arias who was on the outside to get him out of prison. And someone who had found out she was alive and tracked her down.

"Out here is like your American frontier used to be. Rough and rugged," he said. "We even have cowboys and cattle drives."

A sting of emotion passed through her as he rambled on. Ryan had become her hero. The man who'd decided to risk his life with her. And now he'd paid with his life. But that wasn't all. Somehow, he'd managed to grab hold of her heart and started to put it back together again. Watching the explosion had shattered it back into a thousand pieces.

Which was why none of that mattered now. Ryan was gone.

"It doesn't matter what you do to me, to any of us— you will be stopped."

"Not when people find out what happened. It is a shame, actually. A couple of visiting tourists who got themselves into some trouble and had an unfortunate fatal accident on the river. For the most part, travel here is pretty safe unless you run into pirates. Besides, I destroyed your evidence. That leaves me pretty free and clear."

"You'll never get away with this."

He let out a low laugh. "Oh, but I think you're wrong."

She stared off into the distance, toward the remaining pieces of the boat, slowly being engulfed by the dark waters of the river. Who was she kidding? They'd done everything in their power to stop this, but Arias had won. Maybe he was right. She never should have thought she could win against someone like him. She'd tried to save the doctor. Tried to make sure he was safe. But now because of her choices, they were all dead.

But would she really have done it any other way?

"Don't worry. All of this will be over soon," Arias said. "I've got a plane meeting me at daybreak."

Ellie's stomach soured. She fought back the tears as

they walked past one of the houses on the other side of the compound with a thatched roof and a satellite dish and TV. But was this going to be where it ended for her? She glanced around the dirt-packed yard and realized she'd never make it running. Every step felt like she was stepping on a hot poker.

I never really thought it would come to this, God. Ryan's dead. I'm alone again... I don't know how to deal with this.

Because before long, she would be dead as well.

She shoved away the fear that enveloped her. She couldn't let Arias win. They had seen the evidence of his hired hits. There had to be a way to tell someone what they'd seen. She'd heard his orders that had killed Ryan and the others. Maybe that would be enough.

She glanced up at her captor and asked the question she was terrified to ask. "Why do you need me?"

"Because come morning, you're going to be my insurance ticket out of here."

Ryan could feel the heat of the fire behind him as he reached the surface of the Amazon River and drew in a lungful of air. The doctor bobbed in the water a couple of meters downstream. He reached him after three or four strong strokes, the river current in his favor, then started pulling the older man toward the shore. His muscles ached as he pulled him up onto the sand and laid him on his back.

"Dr. Reynolds...can you hear me?"

The older man nodded as he caught his breath. Ryan helped him sit up and checked to make sure he wasn't injured. Beyond a goose egg on his head where they'd tried to knock him out with the butt of their gun, and a few scrapes, he seemed okay. "You saved my live. If you hadn't woken up and smelled that gasoline…"

Maybe he had saved their lives, but there was no time to celebrate.

Where was Diego?

Ryan glanced along the edge of the river between the shoreline and the still burning boat. The last time he saw Diego had been the moment they'd jumped. He had to find him. The boy didn't deserve dying over this. And he had no desire to go tell his mother her oldest child was gone.

"I'll be back."

He dived back down into the murky water, then headed up, just below the surface, searching for him. Ryan slowly turned in a complete three-sixty. Where was Diego?

Ryan swam toward the boat. He could feel the heat from the burning shell, but there was still no sign of the young man.

The knot in his stomach tightened. Arias had Ellie and had destroyed the evidence they'd come for. Which meant he'd failed. Memories of the day Heather died swarmed around him. The call from her mother telling him about the car wreck. Driving to the hospital. Walking into the room and knowing immediately from the expression on her family's faces that Heather hadn't made it.

And then the what-ifs and the guilt that had followed. If he'd driven with her as they'd planned, she might still be alive. All they'd needed was another thirty seconds, and she'd have completely missed that vehicle.

Another thirty seconds and he'd have taken down Arias.

But none of that had happened. And instead, he'd had to deal with Heather's death ever since. And now he was going through the same thing again with Ellie. He should have listened to his father's advice and insisted they leave Brazil the moment he found her in Rio.

Instead, he'd just lost everything.

Including the woman he was falling in love with.

He shoved aside the thought as he caught sight of Diego. He couldn't give up. Not now. Because if Ellie was still alive, he still had a chance of saving her.

Diego was still limp when Ryan lowered him onto the shore. "I don't think he's breathing."

The doctor kneeled beside him and started CPR while Ryan prayed. Whatever happened, they had to find a way to stop the man who'd caused all of this.

Please, God, save Diego.

The doctor continued working on Diego. Seconds later, he spewed out a mouthful of water.

"Diego…"

Diego groaned, then tried to sit up.

"I think he's going to be okay," the doctor said, "but it looks like his leg is burned."

The doctor would have to take care of Diego. He needed to find Ellie.

Diego pulled on Ryan's sleeve. "Where is she?"

"Arias has her." Ryan's worry grew saying it out loud. He had to find her. He knew their plan had been risky, but this wasn't supposed to have happened. It was his job to take care of her. To ensure she stayed safe.

"What do we do now?" the doctor asked.

"I don't know, but I have a feeling they won't be sticking around. I need to get to the other side of the river now."

He glanced at the doctor, knowing what that meant. The knot in his stomach tightened. Arias had tried to kill them, and now he would do the same with Ellie.

"We need to stop him before he hurts her."

"I will." Ryan stood up. "I'm going to find her, then all of us are going to get out of here. It's going to be okay."

"I'm coming with you," Diego said, struggling to sit up. He winced as he tried to put pressure on his foot.

"You're not going anywhere. Your leg's been burned badly."

"I can still walk."

"Forget it." Ryan shook his head as Diego fell back to the ground. "But the doctor's right. You'd only slow us down. Doc, you stay here with Diego."

A motor started up, shifting his attention to the waterway. Arias and his men were back in the boat they'd come in and were heading downriver.

"Ryan?"

"She's got to be on the boat." Numbness spread through him as he watched the boat speed away. "They took her."

"You're probably right," the doctor said, "so how are you going to find her now?"

"I don't know." He kneeled down next to Diego. "You've been watching his men. Where would he go now?"

"He needs to leave the country, but he knows the authorities are searching the waterways." Diego winced as the doctor ripped off his pant leg to examine the large burn on his calf.

"Then how will he go?"

"I was told there's a second camp a few miles down the river, where there is a jeep. There's a road out of there that leads to an airstrip. He knows the authorities are closing in on him and he needs to get as far away as possible."

Which was why he had Ellie. He was using her as insurance. It was the only thing that made sense. Arias was getting out of here, knew the authorities had to be on their way and needed a hostage. And as soon as he was safe... Ryan frowned and didn't let himself finish his thought.

"Diego might be right, but how are you going to go after them?" The doctor stood up. "You'll never catch up to them, especially if they've got a vehicle."

"Maybe not, but at least I have to try."

FOURTEEN

Loud shouts yanked Ellie out of her restless sleep. She opened her eyes and glanced toward the locked door, where Arias had assigned a guard to stand on the other side. She sat up, trying to swallow the lump of fear in her throat. Instead of sleeping, most of the night her mind had raced, fueled by worry and waves of panic. Because everything about their plan to save the doctor had gone horribly wrong.

Arias was now planning to use her as insurance, Ryan and the others were dead and no one else knew where she was or even that she was alive. And even if Ryan's father sent people to look for her, she was hidden somewhere inside thousands of square miles of endless terrain. No one would ever find her.

She fought back the tears and glanced around the empty room. The mat she'd slept on was filthy, but that was the least of her worries. She pulled up her pant leg in order to study her ankle. While it was still sore to the touch, thankfully it was only slightly swollen and discolored. But even if she could run, she wasn't sure it was wise. Arias had made it clear to both her and his armed men what would happen if she tried to run. And knowing Arias, he wouldn't hesitate to follow through with his threats.

She pulled her pant leg back down, wishing desperately Ryan was here with her. Somehow, over the course of the past few days, he'd managed to become the calming force in her life. And for the first time in months, she'd stopped feeling alone. It was as if with him at her side, she could finally see an end to this nightmare, and a time when she was going to be able to put all of this behind her.

But not anymore.

Now any remaining hope had vanished. And no matter how much she longed to see him again, he wasn't going to come to her rescue.

The thought left her panicking. How had Ryan managed to become such an intricate part of her life in such a short time? Lance had broken her heart, but there was something about Ryan that had made her want to trust again. Because as much as she'd fought it, she'd started wondering what it would be like to get to know him better after this was over and they were back home. She could see them together...

But none of that mattered now. Ryan was gone and she was alone. If she was going to get out of this situation, all she could do was hold on to her faith, pray and search for a window of opportunity. But at the moment—with an armed guard outside her room—that didn't seem possible.

She heard the key twist in the door's lock, and she sent up another prayer for wisdom and strength. A second later, Arias appeared in the doorway. "Get up. It's time to go."

"Where are we going?" She didn't move from the corner of the dirt floor. As far as she was concerned, she wasn't going to do anything to make things easier for him. "You said there was a plane."

"You don't have to worry about the details." He touched the butt of his weapon as if he felt he needed to remind her who was in charge. "All you need to do is follow my instructions and keep your mouth shut."

Or else what?

She pressed her lips together instead of spouting off and asking the question out loud. All that would do was make things worse. As long as he kept her alive, there was still a chance of getting out of this. It was the only thing left she had to hold on to.

The sun had barely risen above the horizon a few minutes later, when Arias shoved her into the back of a rusty jeep, then jumped into the front seat beside the driver. Pain shot up her throbbing ankle as she slammed her injured foot against the floorboard in order to catch her balance. Her stomach clenched, and the tears threatened to spill again. She glanced behind her as they left the camp, the sun reflecting off the water. Ryan was out there somewhere. Or at least what remained of his body. She blinked back the tears. She wanted to believe he'd somehow managed to escape, but she'd seen the explosion. No one could have survived that.

She glanced out the window as they followed the dirt track that cut through the jungle. In the distance, a large field burned, its smoke curling upward. Surrounding it was the unending maze of trees. Diego had mentioned the changes in the rain forests. How ranching had brought with it the necessity of fields for their cattle to graze. And how on top of that logging had become another huge business in the region—both legal and illegal.

Their driver slammed on the brakes. Ellie braced her hand against the passenger seat, then looked out the front windshield to see what the problem was. Dozens of cows blocked the road.

She felt Arias's agitation growing from the front passenger seat. "Keep driving. We don't have time for this."

The driver pressed on his horn, trying to maneuver through the throng of cattle, but he was making little progress. She glanced at the door handle. Getting out of the car wouldn't be difficult at this speed, but then what? It was probably more dangerous out there than it was in the vehicle. Dust swirled around the cattle, making it hard to see very far as they stampeded past. And while her ankle thankfully hadn't swelled and the pain was manageable, she wasn't sure how fast of an exit she could make.

Their driver yelled through the closed window. She could see one of the cowboys leading the cattle drive, but he was too far away to catch his attention. With his jeans, leather chaps, Stetson hat and machete, he looked like he'd stepped out of the North American frontier a hundred and fifty years ago. Her fingers squeezed the armrest. Even if she could manage to get his attention, then what? She frowned. There had to be something she could do.

The massive herd was now completely surrounding the vehicle. She glanced in the rearview mirror and saw behind them that another rider was coming toward them in the opposite direction of the cattle. He was partially obscured by the dust, but she could see that this one wasn't wearing a Stetson.

Her heart tripped.

Ryan?

No. That wasn't even possible. She'd seen the boat explode with him on it. Arias had made sure he was dead. She was just seeing what she wanted to see— Ryan coming to her rescue one last time, saving her before Arias killed her.

The rider kept moving in the opposite direction through the herd. She studied him again. Khaki pants, pale blue shirt... She had no idea how, but it was definitely Ryan.

She glanced again at Arias, who was looking out the other side of the vehicle, his impatience distracting him. Ryan was now about a hundred feet from the car. She weighed her options, but it was now or never. She had to make her move. She made sure the door was unlocked, grabbed the handle, then stepped out into the hazy cloud of dust surrounding the vehicle. A large bull brushed against her as she got out, pushing her into the back fender of the car. Flies buzzed around her. The air smelled rank. She squirmed out of the way, praying fervently that she could get away before Arias came after her.

Her chest automatically constricted as she breathed in the dust and started coughing, but she didn't care. Instead, she ran toward Ryan as fast as she could, ignoring the sharp pain radiating through her ankle.

Arias shouted from behind her. She started running faster, more terrified of her capture than the horned bulls surrounding her. Ryan was closer now. Twenty...

maybe thirty feet ahead. All she had to do was make it to him without being stopped by Arias.

Ryan worked to keep the horse he'd borrowed under control as he made his way through the throng of cattle. His only plan was to find Ellie and get her out of here. Beyond that there was no plan. Diego, though, had apparently been right about Arias. Ryan had managed to find a boat heading downriver, where he was finally able to track Arias to this point. He could see the car ahead, surrounded by a sea of cattle. It had to be Arias. And if that was true, Ellie was no doubt with him.

The noise from the cattle drowned out the motor of the jeep. He needed a plan. Except he had no weapon, nothing really other than the advantage of surprise. Which meant all he had to do now was snag Ellie's attention and get her away from Arias.

A piece of cake.

Right.

He sent up another prayer, begging God for the impossible.

His gaze focused on the vehicle. One of the back doors opened, and a second later, he watched Ellie jump out of the jeep and head toward him. His heart stilled as she shouted at a bull pressing against the jeep while he fought his way upstream through the cattle as fast as possible.

"Ellie!"

He caught her gaze but couldn't hear what she was saying above the noise of the cattle. All he needed was another ten feet…another five… The front passenger door of the jeep swung open, and Arias bolted out of the vehicle behind her. But Arias was too late. Ryan reached down to grasp her arm, and in one fluid motion, he managed to pull her up onto the horse behind him. Ellie automatically wrapped her arms tightly around his waist and leaned in against him. Ryan glanced back as Arias pulled out his gun. A shot could cause a stampede, but if the man was motivated by rage and not thinking... Ryan turned his horse around and started weaving through the herd of cattle away from the man as fast as he could. A shot rang out. Ellie's arms tightened around him. The cattle started running to the left, away from the road.

He listened for the sound of a second shot, but they'd already disappeared into a cloud of dust, leaving Arias behind them and out of range. A dozen scenarios raced through his mind. A dozen ways things could have gone wrong.

But God had done the impossible. He'd found her, and she was now out of Arias's grip. That was all that mattered at the moment.

But this still wasn't over. Not yet.

Her arms tightened around his waist. "Ryan..."

Up ahead, a dozen armed men stepped out on the ridge surrounding them. They were dressed in black and shouted out at them to get down off the horse and put their arms in the air.

Ryan helped her off the horse, then dismounted himself.

One of the uniformed men approached them, then held up his hand for the other men to stand down. "Ryan Kendall?"

Ryan nodded.

"We got here as quickly as we could. We're spread a little thin."

"Wait a minute…" Ellie looked up at him, confusion evident in her wide eyes. "What's going on?"

"The cavalry's arrived. These are the good guys, Ellie. They've come to arrest Arias and his men."

"How?"

"I found one of the camps of these cowboys who had a satellite phone. I spent half the night tracking down someone who could help us."

Her smile brightened. "Looks like your hard work paid off."

Ryan looked behind him. One of the men was hand-cuffing Arias and his driver.

"It will be just a matter of time before we get the rest of them," the officer said. "And in the meantime, we'll escort you back to Manaus so you can get home."

Ryan thanked the officer, then turned back to Ellie.

"You okay?" he asked, wrapping his arm around her.

"My ankle's sore, but yeah…" She smiled up at him. "I don't think I've ever been better, actually."

He pulled her into a bear hug, relishing in the fact that she was safe.

Tears streamed down her cheeks as she nuzzled her face into his chest. "I thought you were dead. I saw your boat blow up."

He pulled her in tighter. He could feel his heart racing against hers and felt the relief sweeping through his own body.

She took a step back and ran her fingers gently across the bruise on the side of his face. "I have so many questions. How did you get away?"

"When they hit me I was dazed, but when I smelled the fuel and realized what they were doing, I managed to warn Diego and the doctor and we dived into the water. Another few seconds, though…"

"So they're okay?"

"Diego's leg was burned, but I left the doctor with him. I'll make sure they are picked up so we can get them out of here safely and get Diego the medical help he needs."

She turned toward Arias, who was now handcuffed. "He was going to kill me. He was going to use me as a hostage until he got away and didn't need me anymore."

"I know, but he didn't. You're okay now. We're all okay. And finally—finally all of this is over."

"How did you find me?"

"Diego thought—rightly so—that if Arias didn't take the river, he would head for the airstrip by car. Unfortunately for him, he got caught in the cattle drive, which gave me time to catch up with you."

He brushed back a strand of hair. All he wanted now was a hot shower and a meal, but somehow none of that mattered. She was here, with him.

"There's still one more thing we have to do to put an end to all of this," she said. "We need the evidence, and Arias burned that evidence we had."

"I don't think we're going to have to have it," Ryan said. "Diego took photos. Photos of Arias's men unloading drugs and stolen merchandise. And on top of that, we have the attempted murder of the three of us and your kidnapping."

Ellie looked up at Ryan and smiled. "Enough evidence to put them away for a very, very long time."

Ryan nodded. "Are you ready?"

"More than ready. Let's go home."

FIFTEEN

Ellie glanced out the window of the plane as it flew over the Gulf of Mexico toward Texas. They would then continue on to Colorado, where their flight would be landing in a few more hours. The reality that they were safe had yet to completely sink in. Diego had been admitted into a hospital in São Paulo, where he was expected to make a complete recovery, and the doctor had agreed to return to the United States temporarily in order to testify in front of a grand jury. After a few days of doing her own debriefing with the authorities, she planned to head home.

Ryan shifted next to her in his seat. He was still sound asleep, and it gave her a chance to study his profile. The night he kissed her might have made her look at him differently, but it hadn't really changed anything between them. Now that they'd found their way out of the rabbit hole and Wonderland, things would go back to normal. Or at least as normal as normal could be after what had happened. She'd spend a few days at his father's ranch to rest, then she'd go back to her own life and he'd go back to his.

Imagining anything more ever developing between them was nothing more than wishful thinking on her part.

They talked the first few hours after leaving São Paulo, before she managed to get a couple hours of sleep. But as exhausted as her body was, her mind couldn't stop racing. Telling him stories about her father had somehow felt like a healing balm. She'd felt for the first time since her father's death that she could pour out all her anger and frustration and sadness over the loss. But as cathartic as it had been, complete healing was going to be a slow process.

His eyes opened and he caught her staring. "Hey."

"Morning."

He yawned. "I'll take your word for it. At this point, I'm not really sure if it's morning or night."

She chuckled. "I'm not, either, but it looks like you got a good night's sleep."

"I did. How are you? Did you get any sleep?"

"A little, though I'm still tired. I'm having a hard time settling my mind."

Arias had been captured with enough evidence to put him away for a very long time. His men were being arrested from Rio to Texas, and for the first time in months, she was finally free. Something she was still enjoying getting used to.

"Trust me," he said. "I understand."

"And maybe this is going to sound crazy, but even though I can't ever fix the fact that my father is gone, bringing Arias to justice, seeing him handcuffed, and of course the fact that we survived—along with Diego and the doctor—somehow managed to bring with it a sense of healing and closure."

"That's not crazy at all."

"Good, because I'm beginning to realize that with His strength, I'm stronger than I imagined." She readjusted the pillow behind her head, ready to be off the flight. But at least they were away from Arias and his grasp.

He squeezed her hand. "I could have told you that."

She let out a low laugh. "Seriously, though, back in Rio I kept reading through Isaiah 41—over and over— about how I don't need to fear because He is with me. I thought that was impossible. Then I feel like I faced the impossible and I realized He was there. Every step of the way. Even when things go wrong. He's still there, giving me the strength I need."

"If you ask me, you really are a lot stronger than you think. I always knew that. Stubborn, focused, determined…like that day ten years or so ago when I challenged you to jump off the roof. You stuck out your chin, threw your shoulders back and climbed onto that roof like you owned the place."

She laughed. "You do know that bringing that up doesn't work in your favor?"

He matched her grin. "Looks like I still need to find a way to earn back those brownie points."

"Yes, you do. But I also feel like I'm a different person than I was even a week ago. It reminded me that while I might be stronger, I'm also not invincible. That life is fragile and precious. You can't just sit back and let it pass you by. You have to be intentional in living. I know that's what I plan to do."

He winked at her. "Does that mean you'll let me take you diving one day?"

"Oh…I'm not making any promises." She studied his strong jawline and the curve of his lips and felt her heart stir. No…that wasn't a place she could afford to go. "I think one of the hardest parts, though, of letting go has been the guilt."

The flight attendant came by offering bottled water, but Ellie just waved her away.

"Guilty how?"

"Even if it isn't rational, I wonder what would have happened if I'd met my father somewhere for dinner, and he hadn't been at the house. If I'd shown up a few minutes earlier and scared away the intruder. The only thing that might have changed things was my father going into protective custody. But even then, he wasn't going to let a man like Arias keep him off his case."

He laced her fingers with his. "I never told anyone this, but I'd promised to drive Heather to the store the day she died. We planned to pick up the menu from the caterers, then go over it during lunch for any last-minute details. But I ended up backing out because something came up at work. It's been impossible not to ask myself all the what-ifs. What if I hadn't canceled? What if I had been the one driving? She might still be alive today."

"There's no way you can know that."

"Like with your father," he said. "I'm sure, my head knows that, but that doesn't stop the guilt and the questions."

"Bad things happen, and sometimes we can't stop them."

"And sometimes," he said, catching her gaze, "it strengthens your faith when you realize you have no strength of your own."

Ryan's father was waiting for them in the Denver airport when they walked out of security, toward baggage claim. He was wearing his typical dress pants, buttondown shirt and cowboy boots.

"It's good to see you, son."

Ryan hugged the older version of himself, then took a step back, noticing that while his father appeared relieved to see him, his focus was on Ellie.

"Jarrod."

"Ellie, I can't tell you how glad I am to see you safe," he said, pulling her into his arms.

"And you as well, sir. I owe you my life."

"I'm still waiting to hear the entire story, but it sounds as if the two of you made a pretty good team down there." He took a step back and looked at her. "And you still look great."

"I don't know about that." She laughed. "We don't have any luggage, but thanks to a new set of clothes and a shower at the airport lounge in São Paulo at least I'm finally clean. Or as clean as one can be after a thirteen-hour flight."

"About that quest of yours." His smile faded slightly as his father looked at him for a few seconds, then back to Ellie. "I keep thinking that your father would have been just as irritated at you for not following the plan to return immediately. Going to the Amazon was—"

"I know it wasn't what you wanted us to do, and I am sorry," Ellie interrupted before his father could throw out a string of descriptive words. "And if I'd known how dangerous it was going to be, I would never have gone. I just needed to put an end to this. And I thought the doctor was the way."

"You don't have to explain what you did—or apologize for that matter—though I have to admit that waiting here while all of this played out and not being able to really do anything was torture. But as frustrated as I felt, I also know that your father would have been proud of you. His life revolved around ensuring justice took place, and he would never have let a risk stop him from making sure the truth was made known. It was one of the things I loved about him."

Two men dressed in black slacks and white button-up shirts, and wearing earpieces, stepped up behind his father, their hands clasped behind them. "Dad, what's going on?"

"There's been slight setback," He glanced behind him at the men. "I'm afraid this isn't over yet."

Ellie wrapped her fingers around Ryan's forearm. "What are you talking about?"

"There is a chance that your life is still in danger." His father hesitated before continuing. "Arias escaped from the authorities while they were transporting him to São Paulo."

"What?" Ellie's eyes widened. "You can't be serious."

"Trust me, I'd never joke about something like that."

Ryan wrapped his arm around her waist, trying to digest the information. If Arias was free… "So what does that mean for us? They had a hit out on her."

"The authorities don't think he'll come after you because now there are so many who can testify against him. Instead, they believe he'll disappear…set up in another country. But they're on his trail and convinced they'll find him. In the meantime, US and Brazilian authorities and Interpol are also using their resources to find him."

"But you can't be certain," Ryan said.

"No. That's why I've arranged for security while picking you up and at the ranch. It should just be for a few days, and, Ellie, you're welcome to stay there as long as you want. I've also heard from your aunt, and she'll arrive just before we do. She was anxious to see you, so at least you'll have family with you."

"I appreciate that. Everything you've done for me, but when does this end?" She glanced at Ryan. "What if it doesn't end? What if they don't find him? I don't know how to keep living this way. Running and hiding. Constantly looking over my shoulder. That's why I went to the Amazon in the first place. To stop this. And even without the doctor's evidence, we now have enough to put him away for the rest of his life. But if Arias is free, everything changes."

"I've been assured that this is just temporary. A couple days at the most. But we need to go for now. I've got a car waiting right outside."

They started walking toward the exit, with security now both in front of and behind them. Apprehension settled once again in Ryan's gut. He didn't like this. At all.

"I know this is frustrating," his father said, "but they're on his trail, and I've been assured it's just a matter of time before they find him."

Ryan glanced at Ellie. Just a matter of time. And if

they didn't find Arias? Then what? Ellie was right. She couldn't just keep running.

"What about the leak in my father's office?" she asked. "Have they found out who it is?"

"They believe they're closing in."

Passengers were lining up to their right around the empty luggage carousel that had been marked for their flight. Ryan glanced down at the jeans and yellow-and-green Brazilian national soccer team's T-shirt he'd picked up at the airport before they'd taken off. Talk about traveling light. They'd have to pick up a few essentials, but somehow things like deodorant and an extra change of clothes no longer seemed important.

"How long were you planning to stay, Ryan?"

He glanced at his father as they headed toward the exit, his arm still around Ellie's waist. "I'm not sure now. But I spoke with my boss back at the airport in São Paulo. Told him I needed to make sure all of this was finished before I took on another job."

"Good, because I'd like you on the security team."

"Of course."

He jumped as a buzzer sounded and the carousel began spitting out luggage. He drew in a deep breath. He needed to stay calm and focused, despite how personal this had become.

Ellie looked up at his father. "How did he get away?"

"A man like Arias has deep pockets and connections. They ambushed his police transport vehicle. An officer was killed and two injured."

"I risked my life, Ryan's life—the doctor's and Diego's—and now he's out there again, free and spewing orders?"

"What I do know is that you're safe for now," his father said. "They can't get to you here, Ellie. I'm going to make sure of that."

One of the security officers started talking into his radio as they started out the doors into the perfect fall weather. Ryan glanced around them, his senses on high alert despite the fact that this was supposed to be a safe place. That this was supposed to be over. Because her question had been legitimate. How had this happened?

He turned to his father. "What's going on?"

"Mr. Kendall…" The security guard behind them pushed them toward the curb. "We need to get you out of here. Now."

He held Ellie tighter, hating the loss of control he felt. The enemy might be right in front of them, but he had no idea who or where.

A black SUV with tinted windows stopped along the curb in front of them.

"Get in…now."

A third bodyguard sat in the driver's seat of the running vehicle.

They piled into the three back seats, before the doors were shut and locked.

"What's going on?" Ryan asked.

Their driver spoke into his radio, ignored the question. Someone shouted outside. One of the bodyguards ran back toward the baggage claim.

"Dad, what's going on?"

"I don't know." He leaned in toward the driver. "Should we be getting out of here?"

"I've just been told to wait."

Thirty seconds later, the guard returned, slipped into the front passenger seat and gave them the all clear.

"Sorry about that. We were tapped into the airport security and heard a call come through about an abandoned backpack in baggage claim. Turns out a frazzled mother had accidently left her diaper bag near the luggage carousel. It's over. We're good to go now."

Ryan glanced back toward the airport as they drove away, his gut telling him this was still far from over.

SIXTEEN

Ellie pulled the dessert out of the oven, then took in a deep breath of chocolate. There was something therapeutic about time in the kitchen. She'd insisted on making dinner for the four of them as a celebration. They might not have found Arias, but Arias's enforcer had been arrested and had confirmed that the hit on her had been called off. Which meant for the first time in months she felt free. No more running. No more security. But the long hours of interviews with the authorities had left her both emotionally and physically exhausted. They all needed a change of pace, and a home-cooked meal seemed like a good place to start.

"Ellie…" Her aunt walked into the kitchen wearing a colorful red-and-yellow tunic and black pants. "I don't know what you're making, but it smells delicious."

"Pork loin with a cherry balsamic glaze, homemade yeast rolls and, for dessert, a peanut-butter-chocolate pie I just took out of the oven."

"That," Audrey said, standing over the stove, where the pie was now cooling, "looks amazing."

Ellie wiped her hands against her apron. "I'm just

doing some prep work for now, but I offered to make dinner to celebrate the good news."

"Not having a hit out on you is definitely good news."

Ellie smiled, feeling better than she had in a long time. "I also just heard that they made another arrest. An aide who works for the DA. They're questioning him as we speak, and believe he'll lead them to Arias. Take a bite of the glaze and tell me what you think."

She grabbed a clean spoon from the drawer, then handed it to her aunt.

Audrey took a spoonful. "Wow...this is delicious. Your father used to brag about what a great cook you were. I remember that Thanksgiving I spent the day with the three of you. I wish now I'd done that more often. You were in charge of the pies, and they were the best I'd ever had. If you weren't such a fantastic artist, I'd suggest you open up a restaurant."

Ellie laughed as Audrey handed her the spoon back. "I'm not sure about that. For me I just enjoy the whole creative process of cooking and baking. I didn't have a lot of chances to cook while I was in Brazil."

She dropped the spoon into the sink as another memory flashed at the forefront of Ellie's mind.

"Ellie?"

"I was going to make Dad dinner the night he died. Italian was always one of his favorites. He'd been so stressed over work, I'd thought he could use a home-cooked meal. Thought I could talk with him about what was happening with the case he was working on. He always tried to shelter me from his work."

She hadn't been able to talk to him that night. Instead, she'd found him. Dead.

Audrey squeezed Ellie's hand. "How are you doing with everything that has happened? I know this has been so difficult."

"I'm ready to go home. See my friends and my dog. Find a way to put all of this behind me."

If that was even possible.

"I learned that the doctor who helped us will be spending the next few months with his daughter back in Georgia until things settle down, but thankfully he's okay."

"And the young Brazilian man who helped you?" her aunt asked.

"Ryan's dad has offered to pay for him to go to university. And while he's gone, they're discussing a small business loan project that would help the women in the community start a business, including Diego's mother."

"And Ryan? How does he fit into all of this?"

"Ryan?" Ellie's brow rose. "He doesn't. He's a saturation diver who loves to take risks and leads this adventurous life. I'm an illustrator who prefers to watch romantic comedies on cable. That's not exactly an adrenaline rush. Trust me. He'd get bored with me."

"You're hardly boring, and besides, you seem awfully quick to dismiss any feelings toward him."

She frowned. "For one, there are no feelings to dismiss, and even if there were, it doesn't matter. I have no desire to fall for someone who spends half his time working under the ocean."

"What if you've already fallen for him?"

"I haven't, but even if I fell for him… We were dealing with a life-and-death situation in the Amazon, but anything that might have grown between us isn't real. Not outside that bubble."

"Why not?"

"Because our emotions were running high. Nothing was normal. That's not life. And regular life and the two of us… Like I said, I don't see anything ever working between us."

Because no matter what she might feel for Ryan, it really didn't matter. As soon as Arias was captured, she'd go back to her own life again and Ryan would return to his. Which was what she wanted.

Or was it?

"He kissed me," she said, then regretted the admission. Saying it out loud only made her question her decision to walk away. "But now that I'm safe, and he doesn't have to worry about me anymore—"

"I don't know if that's true." Audrey grabbed a yogurt from the refrigerator. "I've seen the way he looks at you. And the way you look at him."

"You're far too much of a romantic."

"Maybe, but don't throw something away too quickly. You never know when life might throw you a curveball." Audrey pulled off the lid, then dropped it into the trash. "What happens after you leave here?"

It was a question she couldn't quit thinking about. "I guess it's going to be a bit like Lazarus rising from the dead, though I'm planning to return home quietly, with as little fanfare as possible."

"That might be difficult. This is going to hit the news cycle. Local girl, daughter of high-profile, murdered judge, is found alive."

"Hopefully, it will blow over quickly."

All she really cared about was all of this being over. She'd go home. Start over in a new place, start working again and reconnect with friends who still thought she was dead. And do her best to put all of this—as well as Ryan—behind her.

Ellie checked the rising dough of her rolls, then caught her aunt's gaze. There were things she needed to ask her aunt. Things that would help her as she looked for closure over her father's death and everything that had happened over the past few months. "There is something I need to ask you."

"Of course. Anything at all."

"Things have been crazy since we got back with all the interviews with the FBI, and I don't feel as if we've been able to talk. Just the two of us. But there is one thing I need to know. You haven't told me yet what happened the night my father died. Why you believed I was still alive."

Audrey pulled out a pitcher of lemonade from the refrigerator and set it on the large granite island before grabbing a glass from the cupboard.

"Because I saw you."

Ellie's hands dropped to her sides. "You told me on the phone you were there to see my father, but you never really explained why."

"I drove into town see your father that afternoon. As you know, he was stressed about one of his cases and needed someone to talk to."

"He could have come to me."

"He knew that, but he was also worried about you."

Her aunt's answer caught Ellie off guard. "Worried about me? Why?"

"You knew there had been threats. One was toward you. He was planning to talk to you. To insist you leave town until everything blew over. But then, of course, that never happened."

"I wish he hadn't waited so long to talk to me. Wish he had opted for protection for himself."

"There's something else you need to know." Audrey poured a glass of lemonade from the pitcher before answering her question. "Your father and I...we were seeing each other, Ellie."

Audrey paused again as if giving her time to digest the information. And if Ellie was honest with herself, she needed it. Her mother had died over two years ago, and she knew how lonely her father had been since her death. Still, the thought of him falling for her mother's sister surprised her. But on the other hand, they'd known each other for years, had both loved her mother...

Still.

"Romantically?" she asked.

"Yes. It started out as just phone calls. After your mother died, I'd check on him to make sure he was okay. We met a few times for lunch over the next eighteen months or so. At the time, it was never anything serious. Just two friends who'd both lost someone they loved. I never expected to fall in love again. And never with my sister's husband. You have to realize that. But it just...happened."

Ellie shook her head. "The only thing I don't understand is why you didn't tell me."

"I wanted your father to but felt that it wasn't my place. He was apprehensive about what you would think after losing your mom. I told him you'd understand. He'd agreed to tell you that night."

Ellie worked to put the pieces together. Her father had told her he had something to tell her that night, but he'd never hinted that he was interested in someone. And certainly not her aunt.

Audrey held out her hand and showed her the silver ring on her right hand Ellie had noticed when she first arrived. "He gave me this. Nothing official. Yet. We were talking about a possible future between the two of us... I'm sorry. I know this is a lot for you to take in."

"No, it's fine, it's just... It is a bit of a surprise. I wish he had told me. He should have known I'd have been supportive. All I ever wanted was for him to be happy."

"I knew you would have supported us. Now looking back, I just wish I'd insisted we tell you earlier how we felt. Like I said, I just didn't feel like it was my place."

Ellie worked to process through the conversation. Why hadn't her father told her? Losing her mom two years ago had felt like her world was collapsing around her. She'd watched her father struggle with the grief of being a widower, leaving her as more of a caretaker in many ways. But she'd always wanted him to find healing and happiness again. Even if that meant remarrying. Which was why she would have been completely supportive. Why hadn't her father known that?

There was something else she couldn't ignore as well.

"I'm sorry," Ellie said. "In everything that happened I never stopped to think that you lost someone you loved as well—"

"You have nothing to be sorry about. And I know that

your father wouldn't have wanted me to stop searching for you. I guess that was my…gift to him. The one thing I could do. Make sure you were okay. I just had no idea everything involved."

Ellie shoved aside the rest of her questions into a place where she could deal with them later. "What about that night? The night he died."

"I'd driven into town that afternoon and was at his house. I was in the restroom when I heard a noise."

"Arias's man breaking in."

Audrey nodded. "Everything after that…it's still a blur. I heard shots. I've never been so terrified in my life. Your father told me there had been threats against him, but I guess I never thought anyone would actually hurt him."

"Did you see the intruder?"

She pressed her hand against her mouth and shook her head. "No. Just your father lying on the floor. I ran to him and realized he was dead. Then heard the intruder and realized whoever had killed him was still in the house. I—I couldn't find my cell phone. Knew I needed to call 911. But I heard him coming and I was so scared… I ran."

Ellie struggled with what to say. She hadn't realized that her aunt had been so affected by her father's death. And she definitely understood all too well the panic of being in that house with an intruder.

"My arrival must have surprised whoever killed him," Ellie said.

"I saw you leave the house. Knew it wasn't possible that you'd died in that fire."

"Why didn't you just go to the police and tell them what happened?"

Audrey tapped her finger against the glass. "I've asked myself that so many times. But when I realized he was dead… I know it sounds foolish, but I panicked. There was nothing I could do for your father, and I was terrified then for my own life. Worried that they might have seen me and come after me. I couldn't even think. I just ran out of the house and left. I ended up back at my house—seventy-five miles away—with your father's blood all over my shirt before I really realized what I'd done. I was so scared that whoever had killed him would come after me."

Ellie ran through the time line in her head, the memories of the night pressing against her chest. She wished she could forget the vivid pictures in her mind. "I must have shown up as you were leaving."

"When I saw on the news that you were dead, I didn't know what was going on. I thought maybe I'd been wrong. That I hadn't really seen you. Or that you'd been injured. But I couldn't stop looking for you if there was any chance that you might still be alive. But the news kept reporting that you'd died in that fire. There were coroner reports and then the funeral arrangements for both of you."

"I owe you my life," Ellie said. "For calling and warning me that day."

"A part of me never gave up hope that you were still alive, no matter how crazy it sounded. Now that I know you're okay, I just want to put all of this behind me."

She tried to read her aunt's expression. She looked… distracted.

Audrey took a sip of her lemonade. "There's something else I need to tell you."

"Of course."

"I know that what I'm about to say is probably going to come as a bit of a surprise, but... I'm leaving this afternoon."

"Leaving? Today?" Ellie leaned back against the counter. "I've barely been here forty-eight hours. I guess— I guess I assumed you'd stay longer. But, of course, you have your own life."

"It's not that. It's more that I came to see for myself that you were okay, and now that I've done that, I feel like it's time to leave. Besides, you don't need me here. You have Ryan and his father."

"Yes, but you're my only family left now. You spent all this time looking for me. Warned me when you found out they were after me—I owe you so much."

"And I'd do it all again in a heartbeat, I'm just so sorry you had to go through all of this in the first place." Her aunt pulled her into a hug. "I hope you'll keep in touch, and if there's ever anything...*anything* at all I can do for you, please just let me know. I won't be far once you're back home."

"I understand, but I wish you didn't have to go so soon."

"I know, but I've been feeling so restless these past few months. Between the grief of your father and not knowing what had happened to you... But now that I know you're safe, I need to find a way to move on with my life without him."

"What are you going to do?"

"For now, I thought I'd go visit a longtime friend in

Arizona. I haven't seen her for several years, but her husband recently died. She's asked me to stay with her for a few weeks."

"And after that?"

"Honestly, I'm not sure. I thought I might travel a bit. Give myself some time to heal over the loss of your father. Maybe that sounds crazy." Audrey sighed. "I know we weren't married or had even been seeing each other for long, but I still struggle sleeping at night because of the nightmares."

She'd struggled with her own set of nightmares.

"What time is your flight?" Ellie asked.

"Six. Which means I'll miss your dinner." Her aunt glanced at her watch. "I know I should have told you sooner, but I only came to see you in person and make sure you really were all right."

"Let me at least drive you to the airport."

"You don't have to worry about that. You've got your dinner. I can call a taxi. It will be better that way. We can say goodbye here and not at the airport. It would be easier on both of us. Or at least on me." She shot Ellie a smile. "I've always hated goodbyes."

"It's not a problem at all. I'll arrange for a vehicle with Ryan's dad." Ellie pulled off the apron she'd been wearing. "The rolls need to rise and everything else will be fine until I get back. Besides, my father would never let you do that. I don't mind at all. It's the least I can do."

Her aunt pulled her into another hug and nodded. "If you're sure, I'll go finish packing and then we can go."

Ryan stood in one of the stalls in his father's barn, brushing down one of the mares. He'd been back in the United States for less than forty-eight hours, and he already felt restless and confused. A month ago, he hadn't had to worry about what he was going to do the next day. He had his job, his friends, an upcoming vacation... Then somehow Ellie had shown up in his life again, and for the first time in a long time, she'd made him question what he really wanted in life.

"I'm surprised you didn't go to the airport with Ellie." His father leaned against the stall's half door. "You used to avoid working out here. Especially when Ellie came for the summer. From what I remember, you used to live to torture her."

He shot his father a smile and continued brushing. "Maybe I should confess that like every other teenager who had a crush on a girl and didn't know how to show it, I resorted to annoying her."

"I always knew you liked her, even though you were too stubborn to admit it. But today, it seems more like you're avoiding her."

"Ellie?" Ryan took a step back. "Why would I do that?"

"I don't know. I assumed you'd have the answer to that question."

Ryan ignored his father's glare. "No reason, but I'm certainly not avoiding her. Her aunt's leaving and I figured she could use some time with her."

Maybe it was just an excuse. Normally, he didn't hesitate facing a situation head-on. But somehow a few days in the Amazon with her had changed everything, and part of him felt like he was sixteen again with no idea how to approach her.

Maybe that wasn't the main problem. Maybe the

main problem was that he was afraid of finding out. "It doesn't really matter anyway. As soon as the authorities give the go-ahead, she'll be headed back home to her life. I know she's anxious to leave."

His father took a step forward. "I have a confession to make."

"What's that?"

"I had my own reasons behind sending you to Brazil. It wasn't just to check on Ellie."

"Then why did you send me?"

"To give you a chance to move on. You've mourned over Heather long enough. Ellie seemed like the perfect distraction, though I obviously had assumed you'd leave, and not end up captured by pirates." He laughed. "Things might have ended easier if you hadn't taken a side trip."

"So you're telling me this was some sort of…setup?"

"Yes, and no matter what you think, I believe it worked. I've seen how the two of you look at each other. It's pathetic, actually. You're like two lovesick puppies and neither of you will admit it."

Ryan frowned and started brushing the mare's mane. "Nothing's going to happen between us. She made it pretty clear that we're too different."

"I definitely don't buy that. You both have a strong faith, a clear sense of justice and an underlying strength. She's just scared, Ryan. Think about all that she's gone through over the past few months. All she needs is a bit of time and some courting on your part."

Ryan chuckled inwardly at his father's choice of words. He didn't mind feeling like her knight coming to her rescue, but he was pretty sure she wasn't interested in him courting her.

"I don't think that's what she's looking for. Saying we're too different doesn't exactly sound like fear speaking. It sounds like a woman not interested. And while our trip home was good, it was nothing more than as friends."

"Think what you want, but I don't believe it."

"Sorry your plan didn't work, but just because I've healed over Heather, that doesn't mean I'm ready to jump into another relationship."

Or at least that was what he was trying to convince himself. On the plane, he'd been reminded just how much he enjoyed Ellie's company. She was exactly the kind of woman he was looking for. Despite what she'd gone through, there still remained an underlying strength that even Arias and his men couldn't crush. But he wasn't ready to go there. She'd made herself very clear.

"Then when are you going to move on? Because no matter what you say, I think she's perfect for you."

Apparently his father was ready to go there.

"Most people set up friends on blind dates when they think they might be perfect," Ryan said, stepping out of the stall. "They don't send them on a mission together where they almost lose their lives."

"But you're both alive, aren't you? You've been simply surviving for far too long. Hiding down in that underwater pod of yours so you don't have to deal with things."

"I like my job. It's challenging and fulfilling. I'm heading back in two weeks."

These were all things he didn't want to hear. Especially from his father. But that didn't mean they weren't true. He'd been unable to get her out of his mind. He thought about her in the day, dreamed about her at night. And no matter what his head tried to convince him, he knew his heart wasn't listening. But neither was he going to push her in a direction she clearly didn't want to take. Feelings had to flow both ways.

"She's right," he said, stepping out of the barn and into the sunlight. "We're different, and on top of that, my work isn't exactly suitable for a relationship and marriage for starters."

"Then quit your job. Sometimes love is worth changing direction."

"Dad—"

"I get what she said, but I don't believe it. And I believe you'll regret letting her get away."

He stopped in front of the barn. A memory emerged of them racing across the meadow. She'd beat him by a length, and he'd accused her of cheating. It was the same day he'd dared her to jump off the roof. He'd teased her mercilessly that summer and had deserved anything she'd managed to throw his way. But it hadn't been because he didn't like her, but because he had. Something he never would have admitted as a sixteen-year-old.

But today…was he really willing to take a risk at falling in love again? He glanced back toward the house. Because if he was completely honest with himself, falling in love wasn't something he could stop. He was already there.

His phone rang, pulling him out of his thoughts. He checked the caller ID.

"Agent Thomas," he said, "what have you got?"

A minute later, Ryan shoved his phone back in his pocket and turned to his father, still trying to process the information he'd just received. "They found the leak, but they've had their eyes on the wrong person. It wasn't the aide in the DA's office working with Arias—"

"Then who was it?"

Ryan's head spun with the implications as he ran toward the house. "It was her aunt."

"Her aunt? Wait a minute… Ellie just left with her aunt for the airport." His father struggled to keep up with him as he ran up the porch steps.

"I know." Ryan yanked open the screen door and rushed inside. "And we just called off security."

Ryan grabbed his keys off the kitchen counter, then headed back toward the front door. "I'm going after her—"

"Ryan, you need to let the authorities and local police handle this," his father insisted as they both went back outside.

"There's no way I'm going to just sit here and wait to hear from them." He punched Ellie's number into his cell and let the phone ring. "They've got a team on the way to her now. I'm going to meet them there at the airport."

The phone rang another few times, then switched to voice mail.

"Ellie, this is Ryan. Please call me when you get this. Your aunt isn't who you think she is."

He hung up, then pressed the key fob to unlock his car, irritated. "She put her phone on silent this morning when she was talking with the authorities and must have forgotten to turn it back on."

"Do you know where her aunt's going?"

"She told Ellie she was going to visit a friend, but I have a feeling that wasn't true."

"She's probably headed for some nonextradition country with white beaches and stunning diving," his father said.

"She's meeting Arias," Ryan said as he slid into the driver's seat and started the engine.

His father sat down next to him and buckled his seat belt as Ryan peeled out of the long driveway. "I know you went through a lot in Brazil, and I know you're worried, but you can't just race after her."

"That's exactly what I'm going to do."

Five minutes later, they were speeding north toward Denver. Ryan gripped the steering wheel. He felt so out of control. He'd managed to help rescue her from pirates and Arias and get her out of the Amazon all in one piece. He'd thought it was over, but now… This wasn't supposed to happen.

Ryan let out a sharp sigh as he sped around a slow truck, pushing the speed limit as much as he could. "You were right."

"About Ellie?"

"I keep trying to ignore it, but I don't know what I'll do if I lose her."

"Then we better not lose her."

SEVENTEEN

Ellie headed up Interstate 25 toward Denver and the airport in one of Ryan's father's cars. "I still wish you weren't leaving so soon. We could have gone hiking."

"Me, too, but it's time. And you'll be leaving soon as well, won't you?"

"In a couple of days. I'm still needing to rest and re-cover from everything."

"Ellie...I need you to take the next exit."

She glanced at her GPS, confused. "Why? You're not flying out of Denver International—"

"No."

"Then where are we going?"

"You never stop asking questions, do you?"

Ellie glanced at her aunt, taken aback by the tone of her voice. "What's going on?"

"It was never supposed to come to this." Audrey grabbed her purse, then pulled out a handgun "But you were never one to just let things go. I'm not flying out of DIA. And I'm not going to stay with a friend."

Ellie stared at the weapon her aunt had trained on her, her mind scrambling to put everything together. Her aunt had told her she'd been in love with her father.

That she'd spent months looking for her because she'd believed she was alive. She'd even managed to call and warn her in Rio that Arias was after her.

Was none of that true?

What if she hadn't called to warn her but to find out where she was?

Where are you now? her aunt had asked.

In the favela where I work. I was on my way to grab lunch for my team—

Her stomach lurched as the pieces of the puzzle came together. She had to be wrong, but it was the only explanation that made sense.

"You were the leak," she said.

"I told him you'd figure it out, but he said I worried too much."

"Arias?"

Audrey nodded.

"If you're working with him, why come to Colorado to see me?"

"You're in the middle of everything going on. It turned out to be the perfect place to get information. I needed to know who the police were looking at. But they're getting too close to figuring out the truth, so I need to leave. And then when you insisted on driving, well…I couldn't afford a scene back at the house."

"What happens now? You plan to get rid of me like Arias did?"

"That will depend on you."

Ellie gripped the steering wheel tighter as she continued down the highway. She'd like to think that her aunt wouldn't hurt her, but from the expression on her face, pulling the trigger if Ellie didn't do what she was told was definitely an option.

"How could you have betrayed your family? Your sister?"

"It's nothing they didn't do to me. Camille always had everything. She was daddy's favorite, did well in school, scholarships to a prestigious university. She even married the perfect husband, who became a judge."

Ellie shook her head. How had she missed her aunt's anger and bitterness?

"They might not have been perfect," Ellie said. "But I know one thing. They loved you."

"Sometime love isn't enough," Audrey said.

Ellie frowned, remembering her mother telling her how her sister had struggled with substance abuse and money issues, but she'd never given her any details. Never imagined there was a rift between them that would lead to something like this.

Her mind fought to come up with a plan out of this. "You killed my father."

"That wasn't me. I was there, but I didn't kill him."

"But there never was a relationship between you."

"There was a relationship," Audrey said. "At least on his end. He was lonely. Looking for someone who understood him."

"And you—you conned him?"

Nausea spread through her as she noticed the hardened lines across her aunt's brow she'd missed earlier. This couldn't be happening. The leak was supposed to have been someone in the DA's department. Not her aunt. Not family.

"Why?" she asked. "Tell me why you did this."

"He was lonely and needed someone to talk to. And I needed information."

For Arias.

She glanced out at the open yellow fields with spots of trees that ran parallel to the freeway and considered her options. She had to find a way to take back control of the situation, but at this point she had no idea how. "You know you won't get away with this. You might not have pulled the trigger that killed my father, but you're still guilty. If you passed on information, compromised the case and knew about my father's murder…you're complicit in his murder."

"It's too late. I'll be out of the country in a few hours, and I won't be back."

"You never came to see if I was okay. You just came to see what information you could get out of me."

Ellie glanced again at her aunt. While she might not have an escape plan figured out, at least she could get as much information as possible in the meantime. "Where did you meet Arias?"

"We met at an art gallery about a year ago. He was handsome and charming."

"He's a cartel leader who's been arrested for murder."

She'd been taken in by the man. Completely gullible. And somehow, her aunt believed he loved her.

"He ordered a hit on my father, tried to kill Ryan, would have killed me. And that's just for starters. How can you justify that?"

"He was only doing what he had to do to survive so we could be together."

Her temples began to pound. She wasn't even thinking rationally.

"He's playing you," Ellie said. "Don't you get it? He needed insider information on the trial that would get him out of prison, and what better source than the judge."

"No. He loves me, and soon we'll finally be together where the law can't touch us."

If that was what she believed about Arias, then her aunt was more of a fool than she'd first imagined.

"You're wrong," Ellie said. "They have the evidence they need now to put him away for the rest of his life, and there's even a chance he'll get the death penalty."

"That's not going to happen. He's smart enough to not get caught."

"Why call me in Rio?"

Her aunt's expression changed again. "Arias had resources in Brazil but needed a quick way to know exactly where you were. Then Ryan showed up, and somehow you managed to talk him into going to the Amazon and it put a wrench in everything."

And she'd done exactly that. If she'd gone alone, or if Ryan's father hadn't sent him…

There was no remorse in the woman's voice. The aunt whom she'd once eaten Thanksgiving dinner and celebrated birthdays with.

Audrey motioned toward the right. "Take the exit, then head east."

"You don't think Arias actually loves you, do you?" Ellie asked, following her instructions. "He's a man who uses people. That's it."

"You don't know what you're talking about. You don't know him like I do."

She was done with cat-and-mouse games. "What's your plan?"

"Arias's men have a plan. You just keep driving. We'll be there in another few miles."

She scanned the horizon and saw a helicopter coming toward them from the distance.

That had to be her plan. Arias had arranged to whisk her out of here in a helicopter.

"You can park there in the grass about a hundred yards ahead of us. Then turn off the engine and get out of the car."

Ellie followed her aunt's orders, but before she got out, she grabbed her phone and quickly texted the exit number to Ryan. Heart pounding, she pushed Send.

Her aunt flew at her from around the front of the car. "What are you doing?"

"Nothing, I just—"

Audrey ripped the phone from her fingers, threw it onto the ground, then stomped on it. "Don't even think that your hero is going to rescue you this time. But it doesn't matter, really. In another few minutes we'll be gone."

"And then what?" Ellie fought back the tears, but her frustration was rooted mainly from the betrayal. "You'll kill me, too. Like Arias planned. They're going to find him, and he's going to end up in prison, Audrey."

"You're wrong. We'll be long gone before anyone finds us."

Ellie felt the gun pressing against the small of her back as they moved toward an open space where the helicopter could land.

I feel like there's no way out of this tangled web, God.

The arrest of Arias was supposed to have ended all of this. Was supposed to have allowed her to go back to her own life again. But now she'd somehow been betrayed by someone she'd always looked to as family.

She glanced behind her, toward the road, and had no idea if her frantically sent message had gone out. Or even if it had, no idea where Ryan was. Even if he received the message, Audrey was right. She slowed her steps, searching for a way to delay getting on the chopper. They'd be in the air in the next few minutes and she had no way to let Ryan know this time where they were going.

Ryan heard the beep on his phone signaling a message had just come through. "Check my phone, Dad."

He didn't expect the message to be from her. He knew Ellie's life was in danger, but there was no way to know if she knew what was going on. She trusted her aunt and, to be honest, had no reason not to. The fact that the woman was even involved somehow with Arias made no sense to him. He'd spent a little bit of time getting to know Ellie's aunt, and she'd come across as someone who really cared for her family. The fact that she'd betrayed Ellie and her father had yet to calculate.

His father snatched up the phone. "Ryan, it's a message from Ellie."

"What does it say?"

"One-eighty-eight. What does that mean?"

Ryan worked to put meaning to the numbers. "It's got to be an exit."

His father nodded as they passed a road sign. "Yes, and we're almost there."

"Which means they're not going to the airport." Ryan pressed on the accelerator, forgetting the speed limit. "Call Agent Thomas back, and let them know what's going on."

Ryan glanced at the clock on the dashboard. He'd got the call about ten minutes after Ellie and her aunt had left. He increased the vehicle's speed. They weren't that far behind her, which meant it might be possible to catch up.

"He wants to speak with you."

His father put the call on speakerphone. A second later the agent's voice came on the line.

"Agent Thomas."

"You need to stay out of this, Ryan. You know as well as I do what these people can do."

"But you're headed to the airport. That's not where she is."

"I can have people there—"

"Forget it," he said. He could see a helicopter coming in for a landing in the distance. That had to be her aunt's plan of escape. "I can see a helo landing. I'm a couple minutes out. We can't afford to wait."

He took the exit and sped down the road toward the helicopter. Dust kicked up on the horizon. The bird was landing. He pushed on the accelerator as he rounded a corner. There was a large, flat patch of land ahead of them, and a red car sitting on the edge.

"That's them."

He slowed down as he pulled off the road. Her aunt

was holding a gun to Ellie's back and heading toward the bird.

Ryan pulled his gun out of the glove compartment. "Call in the helo's tail numbers and our GPS location so they can track it."

He jumped out of the car. "Ellie—"

"You just can't stay away, can you?" Audrey pulled Ellie in front of her and held the gun against her head.

"Put the weapon down, Audrey." He aimed his weapon at her, shouting above the noise of the helicopter rotors. "There's no way you're going to get away with this."

"Ryan…she's working with Arias. She's not going to just let me walk away from here, and I don't want either of you getting hurt."

He tried to read Ellie's expression, knowing she had to feel betrayed. But instead of panic, he could sense a calmness in both her voice and her eyes.

"We're not leaving," Ryan said. "The authorities know where you are, Audrey. There's literally nowhere for you to go where they can't track you down."

"You don't know that."

"Actually, I do." Ryan took a step forward, weighing his options. With Ellie in front of her, stopping Audrey with a shot was too risky. He was going to have to negotiate his way out of this one. "You need to put your weapon down and put an end to this before things get worse. Before someone else gets hurt and you're held responsible. You don't want that, Audrey."

She shook her head, but he could tell that her resolve was wavering. "Arias promised he'd take care of me and he will. Because you're wrong about him. He loves me. They won't find me, because this is over, and we're leaving."

He glanced at the helicopter. He was surprised the pilot hadn't stepped out of the bird, but he had no way to know if he was armed as well. But he had a feeling that if the pilot was willing to risk his life for Audrey, he would have stepped out by now. He took another step forward.

"Stop, Ryan. I will shoot her."

"She's your family, Audrey. Your own flesh and blood—"

"I made my choice a long time ago. Which means all you have to do is get back in that car and drive away. Because now both of us are getting on that chopper and leaving."

"Ryan. Please. I don't want anyone else hurt."

"You're outgunned and outnumbered, Audrey," his dad said, stepping up beside him with his own weapon aimed at the woman. "The police are right behind us. Ryan's right. It's over."

Ryan caught the panic in the woman's eyes. He should have realized something was off when he first met her. But none of them had expected the woman to be a traitor. He was the one who had encouraged his father to call her aunt and ensure she was there when Ellie arrived. He'd been completely wrong.

Sirens wailed in the distance. The tension in his jaw increased. "Time's up, Audrey. Let her go."

The sirens grew louder.

"Audrey…"

Audrey glanced toward the road. They could see flashing lights in the distance. She slowly bent down, laying her weapon on the ground and taking a step back from Ellie.

He nodded at his father, then headed toward the helicopter.

"Shut it down," he yelled at the pilot. "Now."

The pilot of the chopper turned off the engine, then stepped out with his hands up. "I didn't have anything to do with this."

Ryan grabbed his arm and patted him down before heading back across the open field. "That will be up to a judge to decide."

His father had taken Audrey's weapon and had her sitting on the ground with her hands behind her head. He motioned for the pilot to sit down next to her.

Ryan wrapped his arms around Ellie. "Ellie, I'm so sorry—"

"I'll be okay."

He knew Ellie had to be grieving over the betrayal of her aunt, but all that mattered now was that she was okay. He breathed in the scent of vanilla from her hair, then glanced down at her face, as he held her against his chest. He wanted to ignore everything that was going on around him and kiss her. Because his heart was lost. He knew that now.

His phone rang. He pulled it out of his pocket and glanced at the caller ID. Agent Thomas was calling back.

"Authorities are almost here," he said, "but I've got Audrey, sir. And Ellie's safe."

"Today's a great day, then. I just heard from the authorities in Brazil and Arias was just arrested."

He hung up the phone a few seconds later, keeping

his arm around her. "This is over, Ellie. Finally, truly over. You can go back to living without running."

Ellie glanced at her aunt. "I know, but my mother's sister was involved. No matter what she said to me, I don't understand how she could have betrayed our family like this."

"Men like Arias prey on women like her. Get them to do what they want by flattery. He probably doesn't care what happens to her, as long as she does what he wants. Did she say anything to you? About why she went along with him."

"She fell in love with him and chose him over family." She looked up at him. "We were never especially close, but I believed her. I had no reason not to."

Five police cars spilled into the open space, and the officers exited their vehicles.

"Ryan Kendall?"

"This is who you're looking for," Ryan said. "Audrey Simmons and her pilot."

Ryan watched as one of the officers read Audrey her rights while putting on handcuffs, then led her toward one of the squad cars.

"Miss Webb. Are you okay?"

"Shaken, but yes. I'm fine." She turned back to Ryan. "I owe you my life again. You always seem to be at the right place at the right time. And today, you did it again and risked it all. She could have shot you or your father. Thank you."

"But she didn't. All I care about is that you're okay."

"Honestly, I think I could sleep for about a week, but I guess while I'm sad, I'm relieved more than anything else. I just want to walk away from all of this like it never happened and get back to my own life again."

"Arias won't be seeing the light of day, and sadly, neither will she."

EIGHTEEN

Ellie put on a maroon shift dress, paired it with a jean jacket and tan boots, then looked in the mirror, surprised at how nervous she felt. It wasn't as if this was a date with Ryan. He'd asked her to lunch. Lunch and nothing more. A chance for the two of them to spend a couple of hours together without anyone after them. Thinking it would turn into anything more than that was simply her imagination. But neither could she simply ignore her heart anymore. Her aunt might have been wrong about everything she'd done the past few months, but she'd been right about one thing. She'd fallen—and fallen hard—for Ryan.

Still, she'd also meant it when she'd told him things wouldn't work. He lived on the edge, while she—on the other hand—had experienced enough adventure to last a lifetime.

She glanced into the mirror one last time, deciding to ignore the fact that her nose was red and peeling, and that there were bags under her eyes from exhaustion and a sprinkle of bug bites across her neck. She'd ended up going to bed as soon as they'd arrived back at the house last night. Watching the police take her aunt away in handcuffs, followed by another couple hours of questioning from the police, had completely exhausted her. She'd ended up sleeping last night for over twelve hours. After a long bath and an even longer time praying and reading her Bible this morning, she felt almost like a new person.

Almost.

She knew she wasn't going to be able to just get over what she'd been through. Finding normal again—whatever that was—would take time.

She let out a sigh, her body still feeling the fatigue that had settled in. Especially when she realized how much she had to do. Ryan's father had stored all the things from her apartment in a storage unit when she disappeared. Her best friend, Maddie, had kept Lucy, her golden retriever. She'd need to find a new apartment, but that shouldn't take long. Neither should connecting with her old boss and securing her job back. What she wasn't looking forward to was the buzz she was sure would follow her return, but she missed her friends and longed to be settled again.

And while she was doing all of that, Ryan would be somewhere dozens of feet under the ocean. She'd never make him change. Not for her.

She walked down the stairs of the four-thousand-square-foot house to the entranceway and found him waiting for her.

"Hey. Sorry I'm running a few minutes late."

"No problem." He stood in the entryway in his Levi's, cowboy boots and a rust-and-tan plaid shirt. Her heart raced. "You look beautiful."

"I thought the mosquito bites really added to the

outfit." She laughed. "And I have to say, I never saw you as the cowboy type, but you definitely fit the part."

"I was the one who rescued you from Arias on a horse, in case you had forgotten."

"Trust me, I hadn't forgotten. I guess I just imagined you being more comfortable in scuba gear."

His smile made her heart race. "I just might end up surprising you after all."

Ryan laughed and she felt her heart skip. As much as she'd like to deny it, she was in trouble. "You ready?"

"Before we go eat, I was wondering if we could take a walk for a few minutes."

He took her hand as they stepped outside together. Fall had come while she'd been in Brazil, dropping the temperature. She shifted her attention away from the man walking beside her to the stunning view of Pikes Peak in the distance, wishing she didn't have the undeniable urge to stay.

"I know I've said this before," she said, ignoring the clamor of her heart, "but I owe both you and your father my life. You didn't have to come after me, and you certainly didn't have to follow me to the Amazon."

"Seriously, I'd do it all over again." He stopped in front of the corral. "Especially if it meant reconnecting with you."

She stared past him at the open pastureland, not knowing how to respond. Was he trying to tell her he had the same feelings she'd been trying to ignore?

"I've been thinking of quitting my job," he said, then continued before she could say anything. "Actually, it's something I've been thinking about doing for a long time. I've just been waiting for a reason to quit. A reason to stop running."

She stared at his blue eyes and struggled to breathe. "And you think you've found the right reason?"

"I know I've found the right person."

"You don't think you're going to change your mind? I've seen you, Ryan. You love the water, love your job. To give all that up for me?"

"There are other diving jobs I could do that wouldn't require time away." He pulled her toward him until he was just inches away. "There was a moment when I thought I'd lost you. When Arias took you. I knew at that moment, I didn't want to live life without you. You know how to make me smile. Make me laugh. You're strong and wise. And now that everything is over…I feel exactly the same. I don't want to lose you. No matter what it takes to make things work. And I think—I hope—you feel the same way."

She drew in a deep breath, wanting to believe what he was telling her. "Losing my father, losing the only life I knew…it's changed me. And while the danger might be over now, I still haven't figured out how to deal with what's left behind. Or how to deal with the future for that matter."

"Maybe you don't have to. Or maybe we can do this together. You and me. You're the one I want to spend the rest of my life with. Because as crazy as it might seem, I think I've know this since I watched you jump off the roof that day, trying to prove to me how tough you were."

"And I suppose I did it because I wanted you to notice me."

"Trust me, I did."

He pulled her into a breathless kiss, and all the hurt and fear and guilt she'd felt since her father's death slowly began to melt away, replaced with an assurance that while life might be hard, there was also joy to be found. And she'd found hers in the man holding her in his arms.

Four months later
Fernando de Noronha, Brazil

Ryan took off his snorkel and mask, then made his way back to the shoreline beside Ellie as ripples of sunlight pierced the clear water around them. He'd been surprised when she'd agreed on a diving trip for their honeymoon. But they'd both changed over the past few months. He'd decided to take it easy on their first couple of days out, which meant a few hours snorkeling in the morning, followed by another few hours soaking up some sun on the beach. After that, she'd jumped into diving school and yesterday had finished her sixth dive. With visibility clear up to sixty meters in some areas, they'd already seen spinner dolphins, as well as angelfish, sea turtles and manta rays—all within reach of mile after mile of deserted beaches.

And all time alone with his beautiful wife.

"What did you think about today?" he asked.

"I'll confess," she said, taking his hand as they walked across the sand toward their stuff, "so far this entire trip has been one of the most amazing experiences I've have ever had. Second only to marrying you, of course."

He pulled her against him and kissed her firmly on the lips. "Now I know why you won me over. Saying things like that can get me to do anything for you."

She laughed, then shook out the beach blanket that was big enough for two, before grabbing two bottles of water from the cooler.

"By the way, I have a present for you," she said.

He propped himself up with his elbow beside her and caught her gaze. "If you ask me, the best present I've ever got is right in front of me."

She smiled. "Thank you, but since you've been hanging out with your wife all week—and by the way, I like the sound of that—tomorrow you're booked to do some advanced diving and spend the morning exploring the sunken *Corveta Ipiranga V-17.*"

His eyes widened. "Are you serious?"

"Absolutely."

"What about you?"

"Well, since I already have you to myself this entire two-week trip, I decided I could let you have a morning to yourself." She shot him a smile. "And I have an appointment at the spa, so I think I'll be fine."

"Now I understand your plan. Getting rid of me so you can be pampered."

She laughed. "Exactly."

He took her hand and laced their fingers together. "Do you know that this underwater warship is supposed to be one of the most impressive diving wrecks in the world? They say you can still see things like uniforms and equipment... I'm sorry."

"Don't be," she said, snuggling up beside him. "You look happy."

"I am."

"So am I."

He kissed her again, loving that the fear that had taken over their lives was finally gone. Living and no more running for both of them. And that was exactly what he planned to do for the rest of his life with the woman he loved.

* * * * *

Dear Reader,

Ten years ago, my family and I headed to Brazil for language school, where we spent six months learning Portuguese. While our time was focused on school, I was able to take two short trips. One with my husband to Rio, and a second trip with our three kids to the Amazon. Thankfully, our adventures there were no more dangerous than swimming with the pink dolphins and fishing for piranhas! But it was definitely a time I'll never forget.

I hope you enjoyed Ryan and Ellie's story as they fought to survive in this beautiful country. And even more important as they learned that God is the one who upholds us when all hope is lost. May we always remember that He is the one who will give us the strength we need to face whatever lies before us.

Be blessed,
Lisa Harris

Get 4 FREE REWARDS!

We'll send you 2 FREE Books <u>plus</u> 2 FREE Mystery Gifts.

Love Inspired® Suspense books feature Christian characters facing challenges to their faith... and lives.

FREE Value Over **$20**

YES! Please send me 2 FREE Love Inspired® Suspense novels and my 2 FREE mystery gifts (gifts are worth about $10 retail). After receiving them, if I don't wish to receive any more books, I can return the shipping statement marked "cancel." If I don't cancel, I will receive 4 brand-new novels every month and be billed just $5.24 each for the regular-print edition or $5.74 each for the larger-print edition in the U.S., or $5.74 each for the regular-print edition or $6.24 each for the larger-print edition in Canada. That's a savings of at least 13% off the cover price. It's quite a bargain! Shipping and handling is just 50¢ per book in the U.S. and 75¢ per book in Canada*. I understand that accepting the 2 free books and gifts places me under no obligation to buy anything. I can always return a shipment and cancel at any time. The free books and gifts are mine to keep no matter what I decide.

Choose one: ☐ **Love Inspired® Suspense Regular-Print** (153/353 IDN GMY5) ☐ **Love Inspired® Suspense Larger-Print** (107/307 IDN GMY5)

Name (please print)

Address   Apt. #

City   State/Province   Zip/Postal Code

Mail to the **Reader Service:**
IN U.S.A.: P.O. Box 1341, Buffalo, NY 14240-8531
IN CANADA: P.O. Box 603, Fort Erie, Ontario L2A 5X3

Want to try two free books from another series! Call 1-800-873-8635 or visit www.ReaderService.com.

Looking for inspiration in tales
of hope, faith and heartfelt romance?

Check out **Love Inspired**® and
Love Inspired® **Suspense** books!

New books available every month!

_____

CONNECT WITH US AT:

Harlequin.com/Community

Facebook.com/HarlequinBooks

Twitter.com/HarlequinBooks

Instagram.com/HarlequinBooks

Pinterest.com/HarlequinBooks

ReaderService.com

Love Inspired®